Experiencing
the Joy

Yasmin Peace Series Book 3

Experiencing the Joy

Yasmin Peace Series Book 3

Stephanie Perry Moore

MOODY PUBLIS

CHICAGO

© 2009 by
STEPHANIE PERRY MOORE

All Scripture quotations are taken from the King James Version.

Editor: Kathryn Hall
Interior Design: Ragont Design
Cover Design and Photography: Trevell Southhall at TS Design Studios

Library of Congress Cataloging-in-Publication Data

Moore, Stephanie Perry.
   Experiencing the joy / Stephanie Perry Moore.
     p. cm. — (Yasmin Peace series ; bk. 3)
   Summary: Even though triplet Yasmin faces new challenges after graduating middle school, she never loses hope, grows in self-esteem, and experiences joy, with help from the Lord.
   ISBN 978-0-8024-8604-2
   [1. Christian life—Fiction. 2. Family problems—Fiction. 3. Interpersonal relations—Fiction. 4. Joy—Fiction. 5. Triplets—Fiction. 6. Brothers and sisters—Fiction. 7. African Americans—Fiction.]
   I. Title.

PZ7.M788125Ex 2009
[Fic]—dc22

                      2008047009

1 3 5 7 9 10 8 6 4 2

Printed in the United States of America

Contents

Chapter 1

Another Problem Solved

Thank You, Lord, for working it out for me and my brothers, I prayed silently for York, Yancy, and me. As triplets, we'd been through so much in our thirteen years of life. My dad had been incarcerated, we lost our older brother, Jeff Jr., not even a year ago when he took his own life, and now this horrible fire had put one of my brothers and our next-door neighbor in the hospital.

Even though I was young, I understood that God did care about the Peace family. Things weren't perfect. Though I don't live in a very nice house with both my parents like my friend Veida, at least my own mom didn't kick me out like my friend Asia's mom had done to her. *Lord, thank You,* I continued praying, clasping my hands together and taking a moment to just exhale in the hospital waiting room.

My wild and crazy brother York, who tried to save our neighbor, Miss Sandra, had been successful. Miss Sandra's place went up in smoke, however, but it was such a blessing that we were right next door when it happened. We knew something wasn't right and got her out just in time.

My mom, brothers, and I lived in Jacksonville, Florida. The rest of our family lived in Orlando. Jacksonville and Orlando are only a few hours apart. As soon as Mom called her mom, Big Mama, as we call her, Big Mama immediately called my dad's brother, Uncle John, and his wife, Aunt Lucinda. The two of them drove up and came to the hospital where we were.

When they rushed in to the ER, Yancy and me got up and hugged them both. It was a relief to have them there for support. But that sweet moment was interrupted when my mom ran out from the emergency room looking very distressed.

What was going on now? I had just seen York. Certainly after God had saved his life it wasn't about to be snatched away. What's up, Lord? What's wrong with my mom? Tears were streaming from her eyes faster than a track runner tries to reach the goal. Myrek, my next-door neighbor on the other side, his pregnant sister Jada, who was carrying my deceased brother's child, and their father were there supporting us as well. Mr. Mike had a crush on my mom. She was digging him too and, when he went over to try and console her, she was uncontrollable. I started freaking out as well.

"What is going on?" I shouted.

Uncle John came over and said to Mom, "No, Yvette. Calm down. Yasmin, you gotta help your mom out. You can't go crazy. It's gonna be okay."

A nurse came out moments later and said, "We need to talk to you, Mrs. Peace."

It was three o'clock in the morning and I was so tired, but when my mom returned from talking to the nurse fifteen minutes later, she wasn't as upset but she certainly wasn't happy either. All of us rushed up to her.

"York needs a skin graft. He's badly burned on that arm. It's a third-degree burn and it's causing some kind of infection," Mom told us.

The doctor had explained that, during the skin grafting procedure, he would take some of York's skin that hadn't been burned to help the burned skin. He said that when people get third-degree burns, sometimes they have to get skin grafts.

My mom said, "Medicaid is gonna pay some of it, but I don't know what I'm gonna do about the rest. I don't have that kind of money and he needs that procedure. Lord, You know I don't have that kind of money! And none of y'all can help me," Mom cried.

"We'll find a way," Uncle John said, trying to console her.

"Yeah? How can you? You're moving down here to get a new house. Every dime you got, you hafta put on your down payment. And, Mike, don't even look at me. You're barely hanging on like I am," she said to Myrek's father. "I can't even take care of my own kids. Finally I get a good job and that's still not enough. Lord, You gotta help me," my mom cried.

I just went over and hugged her. I didn't have any money. I couldn't tell her it was going to be okay, but I could let her feel from my embrace that I loved her and that she wasn't in this alone. When she squeezed me back tightly, I knew that someway, somehow we were gonna be okay.

That is, until she pulled away quickly and blurted out, "We don't even have no place to live. Where are we gonna go?"

I hadn't even thought of that. It was time to leave; York was sleeping and there was nothing more we could do at the hospital that night.

Mom was right. As we drove up to what used to be our apartment, only Myrek's was still standing. My mom walked up to what was left of the front door and fell to her knees. The same display of sad emotion that she showed in the hospital, she was now showing. And some of the ashes and dust still burned before us.

"What am I gonna do, Lord?" Mom cried.

"You can't just depend on Him to help us. I'm gonna quit school and get a job," Yancy said.

She quickly got up off her knees and hemmed him up. "Boy, you're about to go to the ninth grade. You're taking honors classes. There's no way I'm gonna have you even think about dropping out of school and becoming some statistic. I'm not gonna have you maybe landing in jail or taking on some road that's gonna lead to nowhere. There's no way I'll have you thinking you gotta help take care of me. We gonna figure this out. The project's management is gonna work this out. Everything is gonna be okay. God's got us!"

My uncle pulled up behind us and gave Mom a key to a hotel room where he and his wife were staying. It had double beds and a pull-out sofa.

"John, you didn't have to do this," my mom said to him.

"Yes, I did, Yvette. I know it seems dark right now. I know you're frustrated. You don't know how you gonna find your way, but we're gonna get through this, sister-in-law. I haven't always been your favorite person, but it's gonna work out."

⋙⋘

Oh my gosh, it feels so good to lie on this bed with the smell of fresh sheets, I thought. I had been so used to sleeping with my mom over the years, I didn't even know what it felt like to sleep in a double bed all by myself. It was wonderful. And I didn't even want to move. I looked to my left and my mom was sleeping peacefully. Then I looked to the right and my brother was a little uncomfortable on the cot, but he was dozing as well. I had never stayed in a hotel before, and though this wasn't a fancy one like the Ritz Carlton that Mom used to work at when we lived in Orlando, it sure was nice.

"I gotta get to the hospital! Wake up, y'all!" Mom shouted suddenly. I wasn't trying to be selfish. I certainly wanted to make sure York was okay, but couldn't I just stay in bed all day relaxing and enjoying this moment?

"Yancy, wake up, boy! Go next door and ask Uncle John to get on up. It's ten o'clock. I need to be at that hospital," Mom said excitedly.

We were there less than an hour later. Yancy and I both were so tired. All we could do was sit in the lobby and hold our heads down, trying to get some more sleep.

"Hey, Unc, can't we go back to the hotel?" Yancy asked.

"I don't know how many more nights I'm gonna have it, son."

"We checked out already?"

"Naw," Uncle John replied.

"Where are we gonna go?" Yancy asked my uncle.

"We're gonna talk to the project's management today. We'll get this all worked out. Just let your mom see that your brother's okay. Then we've gotta try and talk to the hospital insurance adjuster and see how much of this money we gotta come up with to pay for York's surgery."

"I want you kids to come on and eat," Aunt Lucinda said. She had to be getting excited. She and Uncle John were going to be the adoptive parents of Jada's baby. We were excited too, though it was

hard to show it because everything had happened so fast. Jada finally decided that she was going to give the baby up to someone
she knew and someone who was related to the baby's daddy.

It was going to be a blessing, boy or girl, to have a piece of my
brother Jeff still be a part of my life. I couldn't wait to teach that little baby everything I knew. I'm gonna be the best auntie. Having
Uncle John and Aunt Lucinda live in Jacksonville instead of Orlando is really gonna help us make sure we'll be able to do our part.

"Something to eat? Oh, I'm ready," Yancy said, as he got up and
walked over to the elevator. When it opened, Myrek stepped off.

"What are you doing here?" I asked the guy who had been my
best friend for so long. Now our relationship was a little rocky because he wanted to take it further than I did. I mean, we were
friends, so why rock the boat? But I did care deeply for him, and
seeing him standing before me I could tell that he was more than
just tired. Something was going on. Something was wrong. "What
is it?" I asked, when he didn't respond right away.

"We didn't know how to get in touch with y'all. It's Jada."

"What?" Aunt Lucinda asked nervously, as she dropped her
purse. "Where is she? Everything okay?"

"Everything's not okay. They had to deliver her baby last night.
She went into labor early."

"Oh my gosh, Myrek!" I said, hugging him and wishing that I
could do more.

"I gotta go and tell your uncle." My aunt turned around slowly
and went off to find Uncle John. Yancy and I stood waiting on
Myrek to tell us something. This was our baby too. We certainly
cared. But, it was his sister and we didn't want to push. However, I
had to know something. So, I finally asked.

"What's going on? I mean, they're both okay, right?"

"It's a little girl. Jada's fine."

"Okay, that's great!" I said.

"Yeah, but what about the baby?" Yancy asked.

"They don't know. I couldn't stay up there with my dad anymore. He's just pacing back and forth. Jada's all upset about it; she's saying that it's her fault because she didn't have proper medical attention and all that stuff. She even called out for your brother."

"She called out for Jeff?" I asked.

"Yeah. I don't think the baby's gonna make it. She asked him to take care of the baby. She told Jeff to tell Jesus to give her another chance so that she could do better. She'd be the mom that she's supposed to be. I don't know. I guess her medication was makin' her delirious or something. I mean, it was really weird. My dad's all freaked out about it and I just couldn't stay up there any longer." I felt sorry for him. I could tell that he was really upset by what was happening.

Uncle John and Aunt Lucinda came over to Myrek and said, "Please take us up there now." We all got on the elevator and my aunt had her head buried in my uncle's chest. This was gonna be their baby. Just when they got the chance, after trying for years to have a child of their own, they get news that the baby might not even make it. All my aunt kept mumbling was, "Please, Lord, please." She didn't even care if it was a boy or girl. She just wanted a healthy baby, and I so wanted that for them too. But I didn't know what God wanted.

So I put my head back and prayed silently. *Lord, I just seem to be too young to be going through so much. But they say You won't give us more than we can handle. I'm just trying to be happy and find the joy*

in my young life! Why does my little niece hafta be barely holding on?
Do You really need her? We need her too, Lord. Please fix this. When
we stepped off the elevator and saw the grim look on Mr. Mike's
face, I didn't know if God was gonna grant that prayer. I was finding it hard to trust Him.

"It's just a waiting game right now, y'all," Mr. Mike said to us
after we got off the elevator with Myrek.

"You had me there for a minute," Uncle John said to Mr. Mike.
He had noticed, as I did, that look on Mr. Mike's face.

"She's not out of the woods yet," Mr. Mike said before he
looked away.

"Please let me see her," Aunt Lucinda cried.

"Only family can be in there right now. She's in the neonatal
intensive care unit," Mr. Mike insisted.

"We're gonna be her mom and dad. We gotta be able to see
her," Aunt Lucinda said. "Tell them, John. Tell them that we're the
parents. We need to be able to see the baby. We gotta pray for her
and let her know that we're here. Even though we just got into her
life, I've been praying for this baby for years. God's not gonna take
her from me, I know He's not."

"I'm glad y'all are so concerned about the baby, but what about
my daughter? Don't you wanna see her and comfort her? Jada's goin'
through a lot now too. Y'all ain't the only ones." Mr. Mike sounded
even more upset.

I couldn't even stand it anymore. It was just too much to see
adults squabbling at such a time that was already hard enough for
all of us to handle.

"I'm gonna go find my ma and make sure York's okay," I said. When the elevator door opened, I stepped on with a nurse and was happy when the door closed before anyone else could get on it with me. The nurse looked like a girl who used to live in our complex.

"I know you. You're one of them triplets. Girl, you done grown up."

"Yeah, you're Tricky," I answered her.

"Yeah, that's what they used to call me. My real name is Trisha. I had to make something of myself, girl, and get out of them projects. I mean, I know you still live there and all, but keep your head in them books and you'll have other opportunities. It's so many folks I went to high school with that are dead or in jail and ain't making nothin' of their lives."

She just didn't know how she was cutting to the core with everything I'd been going through. My oldest brother didn't even make it out of school and he was dead. York was lying in the hospital right now and the gang that he was affiliated with hadn't even visited. She didn't have to tell me that it was a place that we needed to get out of. But now we desperately wanted to be there and couldn't because it had burned down. It was all just a mess. Obviously, it showed on my face.

She touched my shoulder and said, "Listen, I don't know what you're going through, but I know where you come from and I know you got a lot of odds stacked against you. But, girl, don't you give up. People told me that I wouldn't be nothin' and people told me that I couldn't do nothin'. And a whole lot of the time when the easier way out was the wrong way for sure, I had to pray up and tell God that He said He would never leave me or forsake me.

"I know I need Him to lighten my load. Girl, pray to Him. He will do it. I know you're young and all, but when you got all that pulling at you like you do, that's when you need the Lord. I don't care if you're two or if you're ninety-nine. With your cute little body, I know some of them men that's still over there turning up them bottles are trying to get at you. Uh uh, here's my number." When the elevator opened, she said, "Call me anytime. I work with kids your age at the boys' and girls' club. I'm a good mentor. It's gonna be all right."

"Thanks, Tricky," I said as she winked and walked off to a door that read "Staff Only."

"Where y'all been?" my mom asked as I got off the elevator. "I can't turn my back for five seconds and y'all into something! And where's Uncle John and Aunt Lucinda? They gon' back to the hotel? They couldn't wait? I just would think that y'all would know that I need y'all right now and I gotta be worried about where y'all go—"

"Ma! Please listen," I interrupted her.

"Listen to what?"

"It's Jada," I said.

"What do you mean, honey?"

"Ma, she's in the hospital too. She had her baby last night."

"What? She was fine when we left here yesterday."

"I know but she started feeling pains or something, Myrek said. And they took the baby. It's a girl, Ma. You got a granddaughter," I announced.

"Lord, she had the baby prematurely. Uh!" she uttered. "Let me go and see my baby."

We got on the elevator.

"She's okay, right? Tell me JJ's baby is okay." Mom shook me real hard. "Tell me, Yasmin!"

"Ma, they don't know right now. They don't know."

Mom said, "I was coming to find y'all because York is fine. He's sitting up and talking and even Miss Sandra is gonna be okay. And now you're telling me that my grandchild might not make it? Lord, I just don't know what You want from me!" She pounded the elevator walls. "I sinned a lot in my younger days, I did. And my ex-husband, he's in jail now. You took one son from me. What You gonna do, Lord? What do I need to give You? Take me!"

"Ma, don't say that!" I said. "I need you, Ma. Yancy and York need you too. Please don't say that! The baby's gonna be okay. Ma, you can't break down on me!" I just started yelling as the tears flowed.

There was nothing we could do but wait. So we sat in the waiting room together. Everybody's faces held a different emotion. Hope, disappointment, anger, and sadness.

When the doctor finally stepped in, he had a smile on his face. "We think the baby's gonna pull through. She'll have to stay in the hospital for a couple months, but we've got her stable now. Her lungs are finally breathing on their own."

All of us hugged each other and cried in relief.

When Yancy, Mom, and I went downstairs to check on York, we saw my school counselor and pastor's wife, Mrs. Newman. Mrs. Newman was also one of the coordinators of the after-school girls' group I was in, the L.I.G.H.T. group. It stood for Ladies Impacting Generations Here Today. Mrs. Newman said, "The church is gonna hold a car wash on Sunday. We're gonna raise the funds needed to pay for your son's operation."

Mom couldn't say a word. But I knew just when she was giving up on God, He showed mercy. He came through and helped us out, making another problem solved.

Chapter 2

Lawyer Needed Badly

A week had passed and York was coming home from the hospital. Mom was worried because we still didn't have an apartment. And though I wasn't in on all the talks because I'm not a grown-up, Yancy and I listened in enough to know that many of the people living in Cedar Oaks Projects, the two-hundred-unit complex where we lived, didn't take out insurance. And Mom was one of them.

"You don't need to focus on any of that right now," Mr. Mike told her as we ate some fried catfish at the big carnival our neighbors had put together. It was their way of helping to raise money for my brother's and Miss Sandra's hospital bills. Bone and his crew were even chipping in and washing cars. He wanted to help and my mom wouldn't take a handout so he had his thugs offer manpower instead. They sure knew how to detail. Every customer who drove in for a wash soon drove out with a smile on his face. Then, mean old Mr. Ray, the Cedar Oaks manager, walked up.

"Mrs. Peace, I need to see you now."

"Don't you see I'm eating?" my mom said to him.

"Well, I don't appreciate how you're having all these neighbors coming up to me and telling me that I'm not doing right by you. And if you don't want to discuss anything in private then we'll talk right here and now."

"Oh, no, he didn't," said Miss Lawanda, my mom's friend, who lived around the corner from us. "Girl, don't even take that from him."

Mom lit into him, "Since that fire probably wasn't our fault, the management should help me and every other tenant replace what we lost! Y'all know that most of us can barely scrape together enough money to live on. So having money for insurance is the last thing most of us are thinkin' about. Nobody could even see that little small print about buying insurance that y'all had on those new contracts. Everybody thought it was just like the old contracts we signed when the insurance was already included."

"Well, y'all tenants need to be more responsible. We don't even officially know what the cause of the fire was," Mr. Ray said.

My mom looked away and I could tell that she was a little embarrassed. I knew right then and there that I was going to make that a mental note. When I was old enough to be out on my own I was going to make sure that everything I buy will be covered by insurance. Mr. Mike stood up when Mr. Ray started getting loud.

"No. No, I got this, Mike. I got this," Mom said to him. "After the fire department determines the cause of the fire, we'll have grounds to sue. I know it was some malfunction that caused the fire. Y'all ain't fixed the electric units around here, and everybody's talking about faulty wiring. So don't trip, Ray, 'cuz I might have a lawsuit and you might not have a job since you haven't really been doing yours. So, if you want to go there with me, oh, we can go there." Everybody around started clapping.

"Well, shoot, if you guys would pay your rent on time so we can take care of the water bill, the electric bill, and repair stuff like we're supposed to, nobody around here could complain. But since nobody in this complex went twelve months straight without being late, you need to get out of my face and be thankful that management is lenient with you guys."

Uncle John pulled up and everybody swarmed around the car. It was also a homecoming for York. A news van pulled up right behind them. Then an anchorwoman got out and started interviewing York about his heroic act.

The pretty White lady, who looked like she couldn't be more than twentysomething, went over to York and said, "Hi, are you York Peace?"

"Yes Ma'am," he said.

"Well I'm Lori Anton from Channel Five."

York smiled and said, "Yeah I know. My mom watches your station."

"Great, do you mind if I ask you a few question?"

"No ma'am."

"Thanks. This will be very laid back. I'll edit it at the studio later. We aren't on live."

"Cool."

"If you hadn't gone next door and rescued your neighbor, goodness, I just hate to think of what would've happened. We report so much stuff where young men your age are into things they shouldn't be, but what an awesome story to be able to report how you risked your own life to save someone else's. May we all strive to be like you. And for the town to come out and help with your medical bills is such a blessing. The mayor is talking about naming a day in your honor."

"The mayor needs to talk to the management so we don't get kicked out of this place," Miss Lawanda shouted out and the newscaster heard her.

"Excuse me?" she said, rushing over to my mom.

"Ms. Peace, is this true that you might get kicked out of here?"

"We're poor people just trying to make it, you know. We lost everything and we might not get to stay. I don't know where my family is going to go," Mom answered her.

"Have you talked to the management?" Ms. Anton asked.

"Yes, there's the manager over there," Mom said, pointing at Mr. Ray. He tried to walk away but the newscaster lady called him back.

"Sir, is there a comment? Certainly you wouldn't put this family, this hero, out on the street. There's got to be something you guys would do and make some exception for this family. Certainly, you wouldn't turn your back on them? Would you?" Ms. Anton said, confronting him.

"Oh, no, York is a hero around here and all this is going to get straightened out. I was just coming over to give his mom the keys to another apartment that's been vacant for a while. We had it freshly painted for their arrival. First two months free. It's going to be on the management," Mr. Ray told her, backtracking.

Everyone started cheering. Ms. Anton thanked our family and left with the cameraman. I don't know if God has a sense of humor but the way that whole thing played out was mighty funny. I went over to my brother and gave him a big hug.

"We're getting a new place! Thanks for being a hero," I said.

"Oww, watch the arm, sis! Where's Yancy? I need him to help me fix my plate."

"Oh, so you need a nurse, huh?" I teased.

"Doctor, nurse, lawyer. Shoot. No, I'm just playing. I'm glad to be alive. I went and visited Miss Sandra today before I got out of the hospital. She's supposed to get out soon. She really misses her kids," York replied.

I just shrugged my shoulders, wishing there was something I could do for her. But there was no way I could get her kids for her. I could be upbeat for York. Plus, I was happy my brother was okay and that we were going to have a new home. How cool. I knew I'd keep praying for Miss Sandra though.

⋘◊⋙

Though Mr. Ray gave us a place to stay, we didn't have any furniture. A couple of the neighbors were kind enough to bring over blankets, pillows, chairs, and other stuff just to get us by. Mr. Mike even found a mattress. And since York was still recovering, my mom insisted he take it. Of course, Yancy and I didn't have a problem with that.

Mr. Ray came over and said, "Okay, so it looks like I misspoke on camera. Y'all are only going to be able to stay here free for one month. Since this place was already rented and the new tenant is supposed to move in next month, you're going to have to find somewhere else to go. Then you'll be able to come back once your place is rebuilt."

"So, they're going to rebuild my place?" my mom asked.

"Yours and Sandra's. You started talking about faulty wiring and stuff like that. Nobody wants a lawsuit. Sorry I got to have y'all in and out but I'm trying."

"I know, Ray, I know. And you were right calling us out like you did. We do need to pay our stuff on time. But if we had consistent jobs and we didn't have to steal from Peter to pay Paul, we'd be okay."

Mom went on. "That's why I want my kids to keep getting an education. It's the summertime, and I don't want them getting into any trouble because they got to do better than me when they get older.

"Y'all hear that?" Mom asked us.

She looked over at the three of us and we all echoed, "Yes!"

When Mr. Ray left, Aunt Lucinda and Uncle John came over. She was crying.

"Lucinda, is the baby okay?" Mom asked.

"Yes, she's coming along good, Yvette," Aunt Lucinda answered.

I couldn't believe that after a week the baby still didn't have a name yet. But since Jada was giving her to Uncle John and Aunt Lucinda, she was going to allow them to name her. However, Jada didn't want to sign the papers, or at the least she had been stalling.

"She said she wants to keep her," Aunt Lucinda said, as she fell into my mother's arms and sobbed like a baby in front of all of us.

Uncle John said calmly, "Lucinda, the girl has the right to change her mind."

I couldn't believe Jada had changed her mind like that. Didn't she know she'd be devastating a couple? And, what had changed in her circumstances from when she'd decided to give the baby up in the first place? She didn't have a job and she still wanted to finish high school. But, what was I saying? She'd be able to do all that and raise a baby. It might be hard but she could do it. After all, she is the baby's real mom. If she wanted to keep her now and not ever regret deciding to go her own way, then that was her choice.

Aunt Lucinda had never even held that baby yet, so how could she have such a strong connection? Maybe they could try for another baby. It was just a mess. As Mom stood and talked with the two of them, my aunt mentioned wanting to get a lawyer. But, I knew the only attorney that needed to be involved with this whole thing was our heavenly Father. His counsel alone could make everything right for that little baby.

I was surprised when Mom said, "I'm not trying to take sides here. I mean, remember it's biologically my grandchild and I know y'all are going to be perfect parents. I know it. But we need to make sure this baby is going to be okay right now. She's still not completely out of the woods. Those little lungs of hers have got to get stronger. I just don't want there to be some big custody battle before we know if the little angel is going to even make it."

"Angel. That's what I'm going to start calling her," Lucinda said. "I guess you're right, Yvette. Whether she's with Jada or with us, right now we just want her to be okay."

"Yes stay focused on her health and turn the rest over to God," my mom said.

Uncle John replied, "That's exactly what I've been telling Lucinda. Just wait until Jada feels comfortable with giving the baby to us. We got to trust what's in our hearts. In no way do I think God would honor this if we tried to fight for that little girl. And let's face it, ain't none of us got no money for no court cases no way." Everybody laughed at that true statement.

After my aunt and uncle took us out to dinner, we swung by

the hospital to see the baby. Jada was there with Myrek and Mr. Mike.

Aunt Lucinda went over to them and said, "She's all of our little angel. We don't need to put any negative energy out in the air. We all need to be on one accord. We just want her to make it."

"I didn't mean to break your heart, though," Jada cut in and said. "I'm sorry, I just . . . I just think that I want my baby. I know you guys could give her way more than I could. My dad doesn't even think I'm making the right decision. But, I can't explain it. I just am having second thoughts."

"I understand. Don't worry about explaining it. Just know that we're here for you guys," Aunt Lucinda said as she and Jada hugged. That's when I knew little Angel was going to be okay no matter what happens. Either she could be in the fragile hands of Jada, who had a true mother's desire to love her, or she could be in the nurturing arms of Lucinda, who had prayed to have a baby for years, or she could even be resting in the sweet arms of Jesus with my brother. How could little Angel not be okay? I guess God really was their lawyer. There was no definite decision yet. They were just working it all out.

⊰◊⊱

"Open up in there, Yvette!" Miss Lawanda pounded on our door around midnight.

"Ma, wake up," I said, "Miss Lawanda's at the door."

"Whatever. If we don't answer she'll go on and go away. She might not have nothing better to do, but I need some sleep. We gotta get up early in the morning."

As I went to lie back down, "Get up, Yvette," I heard her say through the door. "This is important, come on now." Because she sounded like she had something urgent to say, I went on and answered the door.

"Thank you, girl, where's your mama?"

"She's right back there, Miss Lawanda," I said, noticing that she had Miss Sandra with her too. I was happy to see Miss Sandra up and out of the hospital.

"Hi, Miss Sandra," I greeted her.

Miss Sandra hugged me and said she was glad to see me.

"Sandra, girl, what you doing out this late?" Mom asked as she came through the hallway.

"She's staying with me while they fix her place," Miss Lawanda said. "Yvette, Sandra wants to talk to you about her kids. She's been keeping me up all night and you know I need to get my beauty rest. I told her that she needed to come over here and talk to you."

"Oh, thanks," my mom said sarcastically.

Miss Sandra said, "I'm sorry, Yvette."

"It's okay. I know it's late, but it's okay," Mom replied.

Miss Sandra continued, "No. No, I'm sorry for everything. I still don't even know what happened. I just remember being really depressed and upset that my babies were gone. I was smoking a cigarette and the next thing I knew the place was up in flames. Your baby could've died, and I know I haven't been the best mama but I could've got your son killed."

"It's okay. It's okay," my mom said. I went toward the bedroom. The temporary place where we were living was a one bedroom, and Yancy and York were sleeping in there.

"What's all that noise out there?" York asked.

"It's Miss Sandra. She wants to come and thank you," I said.

"We already talked. I'm sleepy. Tell her it's cool," York said.

"Boy, get up!" I yelled.

"He said he's tired, Yasmin," Yancy said, taking up for York. It was actually weird that since York had gotten out of the hospital, he and Yancy had been extra tight. I had always played mediator for so long, I wasn't used to them getting along so well. It was actually scary and I was a little jealous.

"Okay, okay. Don't bite my head off. I'll tell her y'all are asleep." I shut the door. I went back to the living room to where Mom was talking with the two ladies. Miss Lawanda had a million rollers of all different colors in her hair, and I noticed that Miss Sandra's face was discolored from the burn marks.

"We got to find a way to help me, Yvette. You're smart with all this stuff. You made it possible for us to even have them rebuild our place. And you know that the whole thing was my fault."

"Nobody knows that for sure, Sandra; even you're saying you can't remember what exactly happened. We've all paid enough. I'm just glad we'll finally have our roof back over our heads soon," Mom replied.

"I just want to see my kids. After all I've been through, the Department of Children and Families won't let me. They won't even tell me where my babies are. They're saying that I have to go to court. I got to find somebody who can represent me. I can't lose my kids. The only thing that made me want to get through all of this is wanting to hold those babies in my arms."

I hadn't thought about Randi and Dante in a while. So much had been happening in my own life. My world had been so upside down, I'd never even stopped to think if theirs probably was too. If they're not even together in the same home, then I know they're both terrified.

So I prayed. *Lord, please protect Randi and Dante. Don't let them be scared, Lord. May whoever has them really be good people. Thank You, Lord, for watching over all of us, and help Miss Sandra get herself on track so she can get them back. Also, Lord, thank You for allowing York and Yancy to get along better, but I need You to help me not let the green-eyed monster get me all worked up over their male bonding. Thanks, Lord. Amen.*

"Yasmin, girl, say good night," Mom said.

"Good night, Miss Lawanda and Miss Sandra."

"Thanks again, Yvette," Miss Sandra said.

"Girl, I'll see you tomorrow," Lawanda said. "I gotta come over here and tell you what's going on with 15A and 15C."

"Girl, bye, you know I don't need any gossip," Mom said, shaking her head.

"Oh, child, trust me. You're gonna wanna hear this." When she shut the door, Mom came over and gave me a hug.

"What's this for?" I said.

"Just for you being you. You're being a good girl with so much going on right now. I'm just proud of you, and I love you. I just wanted to tell you that."

"Thanks, Ma," I said actually amazed. Maybe God was giving me time to bond with my mom. Though we'd been very close for so long, we were growing apart as I was becoming a teen.

"I hate that you have to be grown up," she said.

"Ma, I'm not a baby anymore. I'm a teenager."

"I know, but we have such cramped space that you got to be in on grown-up conversations more than I want you to. But, you do stay back. You're like a fly on the wall. Sometimes I forget you're even around. But, I know all the stuff you're soaking up has got to be freaking you out: a teenage mother wanting to keep her baby and a mother who lost her babies, wishing that she had a second chance to do better.

"I don't know, Yasmin, I wish I could shield you from so much drama. The only thing I pray is that all this stuff that you're hearing about will make you want to do right. I sure don't want you to sink into a horrible trap, or sit in jail like your dad, crying 'lawyer needed badly.'"

Chapter 3

Whatever
You Say

"Okay, Ma, I got you," I said, as she became overly emotional with me that night. I knew she had high expectations for me; I had big dreams for myself too. And though she and my dad weren't married anymore, I didn't want her to look down on him. Being in jail wasn't a great thing, but he told me how sorry he was about that.

I didn't know when he'd be getting out, but I knew he was up for parole soon and that meant he had a chance to start over. Mom was still upset with him. However, I was hoping that if he needed us we'd find a way to show him love.

"All right, well, it's late. You can just go on back to bed. We're gonna go to church in the morning. Then Monday you go back to school, for what—a week?"

"Yes, ma'am. I'm getting ready to graduate from the eighth grade."

"You and my other two babies. Where does the time go?"

"Ma, we'll always be your babies," I said, as I gave her a kiss on the cheek.

"You got that right." We actually hadn't been to church in over a month. York didn't want to go. He was still in pain but Mom was so thankful that he was alive. She made sure we were not only there early, but sitting on the front row as well.

Pastor Newman acknowledged us, and a lot of church members during the fellowship time came up and shook our hands. It was actually pretty powerful when Mom was asked to get up and say a few words. She thanked the church for their tremendous support.

But it got overly emotional for me when Pastor Newman started preaching. He said, "I want to talk to you all about the prayer of Jabez. If you're at a place in your life where you just want something good to happen, you want to take things to a new level, or you need a breakthrough, then this particular story in the Bible is for you."

I sat up on the edge of my seat. Though I wasn't an adult, Mom was right. I had been through a lot with a bunch of obstacles put in my way. And I was ready to overcome them all. What did Jabez pray that made his life better?

Reverend Newman continued, "God is a sovereign God, and He is worthy of our reverence and respect. But some of y'all just don't know how to pray. You can talk to your girlfriend on the phone. You can complain to everybody in the world about this or that, but when you go to talk to God, you're just not being real with Him. You just don't let it all out. And see, Jabez was real. He asked the Lord to enlarge his territory and to bless him indeed."

I knew then that I needed to stay connected with the Lord. I didn't know what was awaiting me in high school, but I knew if I needed Him to help me get through middle school, I certainly was gonna need Him on the next level. Because so much of my eighth-grade year was sheer heartache, I was real with God to get through it and He answered.

At that moment I felt compelled. I wanted to read the Bible more. Sometimes I didn't know which way to go or what to do, but I would pray. I would talk to God. But right there in His Word was a road map and though I might not be able to understand everything, this good church was ready to help show me the way. Yeah, I was like Jabez. My relationship with the Lord was real.

❧

"Mom, I'm tired of hospitals," York said when we stopped by to check on little Angel.

As we entered the elevator, Mom said, "This is my grand-daughter and I want to see her. I want to make sure she's all right. And y'all might think y'all grown, but you ain't grown. So, Yasmin, push number seven and let's go see about this baby."

The three of us stayed quiet on the elevator, knowing that she still called the shots. One thing for sure, we had a strong mama who had no problem keeping us in line.

I didn't know what to make of it when the elevator door opened and we saw Aunt Lucinda standing there in tears. Mom mumbled, "Now, she's gonna just have to stop coming up here. She knows that baby is not hers. She keeps getting herself all worked up, knowing she ain't gonna be able to have that child. I mean, we can give her an update on the baby!"

"Ma, maybe the baby ain't all right," York said to her.

"Boy, hush your mouth. They would've called me." Mom

opened up her arms, switched her tone and said, "Oh, Lucinda, sweetheart, I know it's hard, girl. But don't cry about it."

"I was just about to call you," Aunt Lucinda said, as she wiped at her tears.

"Wait, you were about to call me?" Mom said, realizing York's angle could be correct. "Angel's okay, right?"

"She's absolutely precious and growing stronger by the minute."

"Okay, so what's got you in tears?" Mom asked.

"Jada," my aunt said, smiling widely and showing all her beautiful teeth. "She just sent us some papers and said we would be able to keep the baby. John and I are gonna be Angel's parents after all."

Mom hugged Aunt Lucinda. Watching their embrace was so refreshing. My mother was truly elated and Aunt Lucinda couldn't maintain her joy. I spotted Jada looking at them from further down the hallway. I walked down to meet her and said, "Are you sure about this?"

"Sure about what?" she said, brushing me off as if I knew nothing.

"Come on, Jada. You really wanna give the baby up? I'm not trying to stir up anything, but you were so sure a couple of days ago that there was no way you could do this."

"I realize that I love her and even though I want to keep her, I'm showing her more love by giving her a home. I'll be able to babysit, visit her from time to time, and pray for her always. People say actions speak louder than words. Your uncle and aunt, they've both shown me that they really want Angel to be theirs, and I really felt God say that it's okay for me to let her go in that way. I know that I heard from Him."

"Then, all right, girl. You know whatever He says goes."

"Yeah," Jada said, as we smiled at each another.

⤜⟡⤏

"We are so glad that your brothers are okay," Asia said to me as we gathered with Perlicia, Veida, and a couple other girls in the L.I.G.H.T. group. We were waiting for our session to start.

"I hate that I couldn't get in touch with y'all," Veida spoke up.

"Yeah, with us not owning any cell phones and our house up in flames, that was pretty impossible," I replied.

"I heard that lady's children died. Is that true?" Perlicia asked.

"No way!" I said quickly. "You can't believe everything you hear."

"The folks who told me about it said they couldn't find her kids nowhere," Perlicia continued as if I had wrong information.

"That's because her kids were already somewhere else."

"She lost them?" Asia asked.

I didn't want to get into all of that. It wasn't my business, which was so weird. My mom had already pre-warned me that some stuff wasn't my concern. I could only pray for Miss Sandra. She had enough bad news on her plate. She didn't need me adding any rumors to fan the flame.

"I tried to talk to Yancy about it earlier today in school but, of course, he went the other way," Veida said in an upset tone. I didn't know how to take her comment; I mean, she had been my brother's girlfriend until she cheated on him. And though there was a lot going on in our own personal household, her behavior made her trip beyond the level that was cool. It couldn't be excused and I understood why my brother was through with her.

"I wanted to make sure York was okay too," Asia said. "I couldn't come to that big ol' barbeque that the community had. My mom invited me over for dinner that day."

"Oh my gosh, girl! That is so great," I said to her, all excited. Asia and her mom had been through it. There were issues with Asia and her stepfather not getting along and when her mom had to make a decision, Asia was not her choice. But it looked like things were getting better, and that made me feel good hearing her good news.

"It wasn't like she invited me to come back home to stay. He was out of town," she explained.

"Well, at least you and the parent you got issues with are talking. Ever since my dad found out my mom was cheating on him, he moved out of the house," Veida interjected.

"Are you serious?" I asked, realizing it had been a while since I had participated in real girl talk. Although I had a lot of drama going on in my life, my friends did too.

Perlicia was quick to say, "Well, my life ain't as bad as y'all's. My dad might not have the best job as a trash man, but it's a steady job. Besides, he and my mom have been together for eighteen years, and they still act all in love. I actually get tired of hearing him say how much he loves all of us."

Veida, Asia, and I looked at her like she was tripping. We wished our house was that stable. I guess the grass always looks greener . . .

"Just tell York that I said hi. We only got a few more days of school left," Asia said.

"Yeah, my mom is just letting him chill. But since we didn't have a hurricane or tornado and got those extra days to make up last week, he actually could've come. But he's still in a lot of pain and that medication wouldn't let him get up this morning."

"I wish that would've been me," Perlicia said.

Asia cut in, "No you don't, girl. He's gonna have a scar."

"He's a boy. He don't care nothing about that," Perlicia commented.

"Yeah, he does. York cares a ton about his appearance. Remember, he's the one that stole from that store just to have new clothes," Veida blabbed out.

I looked at her like, *How do you know all that?* But I forgot that she was dating my brother at the time. Yancy's big mouth was happy to tell York's misfortune. I gave Veida a look like, *that was private family stuff. Did you have to open your mouth?*

Then she quickly realized she had overstepped and said, "I'm sorry!"

At that moment, the two sponsors, Mrs. Newman, my counselor and pastor's wife, and Miss Bennett, my English teacher, walked in. Miss Bennett said, "Welcome, ladies. It feels like we just started this group yesterday. And now most of you are going on to ninth grade."

"We gotta continue it!" Asia shouted out.

Mrs. Bennett added, "We'll probably continue it here, but you girls have grown. I've been talking to a lot of you, and I think the only lesson left for us to give you is that of self-esteem. Over the past weeks, we had many different people come before you and speak on various topics."

Mrs. Newman spoke up, "Today I'm gonna talk to you guys about how I was diagnosed with severe depression when I was in college."

All of us looked around at each other. She was the pastor's wife. No one could imagine her down. She rolled up her pants leg, turned her left thigh toward us, and showed us a severe scar. It actually looked like a bear had clawed through the middle of her skin and left its tracks to prove to the world it was a fierce creature.

As she gestured toward it, she said, "Long story behind that mark. The quick version is that when I was your age I had just gotten a moped. One of the stipulations my father put on me was that I couldn't ride it when he wasn't around. And whenever I rode it, I needed to make sure I wore pants. Well, he was gone for a long time one day and I was anxious to ride. Not only did I want to ride, I had a friend that wanted to feel the breeze. It was hot and I was wearing shorts; I told her to hop on. I wasn't used to carrying someone else. So, as soon as the rocks came my way, we went skidding down a road and my leg got burned on the motor."

She didn't have to tell us, but the way she looked at us let me know that the first lesson was: do what your parents say or there will be consequences you can't control.

But then she surprised all of us by saying, "I went to college and tried out for cheering. My burn was still there and people said all kinds of mean-spirited things about me. Saying that I had ugly legs was the nicest thing. Soon I started believing all that stuff. So, I went to counseling and finally got some help. But, I didn't have a breakthrough until the doctor made me realize that it wasn't the scar on the outside that was holding me back, it was all the stuff on the inside that I needed to release."

As we listened intently, Mrs. Newman continued with her wise words. "See, people are always gonna say stuff about you. You might not ever feel like the prettiest girl in your school or the richest. But, as long as you believe in you, as long as you're excited about who you are, you take a lesson from the ugliest scars of life and make them help you become stronger. Only then you'll soar. Sticks and stones will break your bones, but words, young ladies . . . Don't let the negative mean words of others or even those words that you may say to yourself hold you back. If you ever get so down, seek help to lift you up. Feeling horrible for any length of time is unhealthy. Don't be weighed down by negative thoughts. Release all of that, and from here on only speak positive thoughts to yourself to be the best you that you can be."

⋘⋙

It was finally eighth-grade graduation day. Our gymnasium was decked out. I didn't even notice it to be the same place. Carpet was rolled out in the middle for us to walk down the aisle, plants and flowers decorated the podium, and parents were all over the bleachers with other family members and friends. And, all 152 of us eighth graders were beaming with pride. Our school was the one in the county that was known not to send many students on to high school. But, in this particular year, 100 percent of those enrolled in the eighth grade were going on to high school.

When that fact was announced, even though everyone knew it, we just all got up, shouted, and felt really proud of each other. The first Black superintendent of Jacksonville approached the podium to address us. We watched history in the making when he stepped toward the microphone. I looked to my left and saw Yancy. I was proud of him because he had a gold rope around his neck; he was graduating with honors.

Even though there were times throughout the school year that he didn't want any part of the smart class, I could tell as his eyes watched the man standing at the podium, Yancy was feeling that he could be like him one day. He could be a doctor or whatever he wanted to be. He could make history.

And then I looked to my right, and even though neither York nor I had anything extra around our necks, we were in the house. York had passed his remedial course and was going to high school on target. He had literally and figuratively come through the fire, and I could see his eyes held hope. Hope that since he had made it through this part of the race, now he could continue on and change the course of his life by not making any bad decisions. As a town hero, he could use that as a springboard to do more great things.

"Well, today I stand here in front of a group of winners. I really don't feel like I need to say anything more because of the fact that each one of you is sitting in front of me, and that means everything has already been said," Dr. Tomlin began. "Who said you wouldn't make it? People say, 'Maybe this is the school we need to close down. Those kids over there aren't trying to learn, they're not trying to be anything; they're not trying to do better.'

"Young people, you have proved that saying is wrong. As you are sitting in these seats today, it says that you want to become a doctor, you want to become a lawyer, you want to become an architect; you want to become someone great. And just like people told me that I wouldn't have this job, I'm here today to tell you, forget what people say. Keep on believing in you."

I looked over at York and he winked at me. Yancy nudged me in the arm. The three of us were triplets and we were feeling positive and strong together. We were on one accord, wanting the best for each other.

Finally, Mom had let it be known where she was sitting. She

was on the top row of the sixth bleacher alongside my Uncle John and Aunt Lucinda.

Big Mama had called us before we came to the ceremony and apologized that she couldn't be here. She just didn't sound like herself. She said that she didn't feel well. I was happy that we made her proud. She dropped out of school in the eighth grade and now we are a part of her legacy, realizing her dreams.

Dr. Tomlin continued, "Take this milestone in your life and build on it. Like the story of the three little pigs, I know you all are big eighth graders, but you guys remember it from when you were back in kindergarten. Don't build your future on straw or wood. If you put only a little work in when you get to high school next year, it won't be enough. If you hang with the wrong crowds or simply tell yourself negative things, it will begin to sink in and hold you back.

"Instead, build your future on bricks and mortar. Use this summer to check out library books and spend some time reading. Find someone to mentor you in the career you might be thinking about entering. Be serious about your studies from day one of high school and don't look back until you graduate four years from now.

"Yes, folks, this is only the beginning. But can't you see that you can make it? You can do it. You all are the bomb. If you tell yourself you're nothing, then you'll be nothing. But, if you tell yourself that you can be the president of the United States and the most intelligent person in the world, then you'll be something. You can make all your dreams come true and you will become whatever you say."

Chapter 4

Summer Is Here

*I*t was June and it was past hot in Florida. A scorching ninety-four degrees and everybody was ready to have some fun. Two weeks had passed since we'd been out of school and gotten kicked out of our temporary apartment. Now we had to live with Uncle John, Aunt Lucinda, and little Angel.

Yes, she was home and, of course, in the beginning everything was rosy. But, it only took twenty-four hours for that to wear off. Then we all were getting on each other's nerves in what at first seemed like a dream home. A three-bedroom, two-and-a-half-bath home was still too cramped for three adults, three teenagers, and a screaming baby.

"Yvette, I'm sorry, girl. It's just with this baby, I'm all overly protective. Please have your kids wipe down the sinks and the bathtubs. I just want to keep my house sanitary," Aunt Lucinda said.

"Girl, it ain't like that baby is going to be using the bathroom anytime soon," Mom told her.

"I know, I know. I just want to keep it nice for her. And the boys like to poke her cheeks sometimes when they haven't washed their hands. You know, she's still a preemie."

Of course, Mom was offended. And when she told my brothers, York said he wouldn't touch the baby if she paid him, and Yancy said he was going to touch the baby just to tick her off. Mom wasn't even opposed to that.

"Now, I done had four babies," she vented to us, "I know what not to do around young kids."

That was only the first time they argued. A couple days later, Mom came in at 11:40 p.m. Aunt Lucinda was waiting by the door. My brothers and I were in the back room watching TV until we heard their voices elevating.

"I'm not setting a bad example for my kids. My kids are about to be fourteen years old. They know I'm grown and got a life. You need to get with your man who is back there. I'm single. I can go out if I want," Mom argued.

"Yes, but this is my house. And I have a baby and a chime," Aunt Lucinda responded.

"Well, turn the chime off. It's just an alarm. I've been to y'all's old house. Don't try to front like you all high and mighty."

"Well, this is my house and my rules, Yvette," Aunt Lucinda said firmly.

"Lucinda, if you're gonna go there with me, then I'll pack up my kids and leave right now."

The three of us were peeking around the corner, ready to step in at any minute and break it up. Mom and Aunt Lucinda never seemed to be the best of friends because Mom wasn't that fond of Uncle John for the longest time. But over the last few months they had bonded and now that bond was breaking apart. Uncle John came from the back of the house.

He said, "Y'all are acting silly. Y'all know we got kids in this house, the baby's asleep, and y'all yelling and fussing like that."

"You better check your wife," my mom said to him. "You know what? I don't even have to deal with this," Mom said, flying around the corner.

"What are the three of y'all doing, being nosy? Unless y'all have a job and an apartment, then I suggest y'all get out of my face and go pack your stuff."

"Ma, come on. We can work this out. Where are we going to go?" Yancy said, wanting to keep the peace with Uncle John and his wife.

"Whatever, man, he's too strict. Every time I dial somebody he wants to know who I'm calling. I mean, he's cool and all but it ain't like he's my dad," York chimed in.

We didn't have suitcases because most of what we had was burned up in the fire. But we did have some clothes that folks had given us. Mom got a trash bag and started stuffing it.

"What? I'm not going to compromise the way I want my house run," Aunt Lucinda yelled. "I didn't tell her that she had to go anywhere. It's her choice and her decision, but don't make me feel bad because I want this place to be a safe haven for my baby."

"You're just going overboard, honey. Everybody knows how to respect that baby."

"Maybe you're right, John. But, if she ends up going back to the hospital, I just would feel—" Aunt Lucinda started.

Mom looked over at me. "Like I'm going to do something to send the child to the hospital? Let me get up out of here. Black people get a little something and lose their minds."

I couldn't believe my mom was talking to me like I was her girlfriend. She was so hot that I guess even I would do.

Then she started to face reality. "What am I doing? What am I saying? I don't have nowhere to go and take y'all," she said, sitting on the mattress. "It's nighttime and it's burning up outside. What am I going to do? Put us on the streets? What am I thinking? Times when you live with other people, you got to live by their rules. I'm not being a good example for my own kids." She put her head down and the tears welled up.

I went over, stroked her back and said, "Mom that's not true. We love you. You work hard and ain't nothing wrong with wanting to have a little fun."

"Yeah, but—" she started to reply. Then my uncle knocked on the door. I went over and let him in. I could see my mother was a little upset at herself.

"Yvette, please, we don't want you to go anywhere," Uncle John said.

My mom replied, "Well, that's good. My pride got in the way. It ain't like I really got somewhere to go. I need to abide by your wife's rules. What was I thinking? Tell her to write me a list. I'll try to be out of y'all's hair soon, John."

Aunt Lucinda slid through the door, came over, and sat beside Mom. "Yvette, you got good kids. I'm so sorry if I made you think that y'all weren't good enough to be here, or y'all were doing something wrong and needed to go. And you're right, I can't tell you how to come and go. Even though you're in my place, this is your place too. We're family. Forgive me for being overly protective.

Being a first-time mom and not wanting to mess up, that's all. Maybe this heat just got me flustered."

Mom hugged her and said, "Yeah, maybe I'm a little hot under the collar with summer here too. We're cool, though."

I went and told my brothers. Yancy smiled and York hit his duffle bag with his arm that was healing and yelled. Yancy and I laughed. Family was crazy, but family was all we had and we needed to learn how to live together.

The party was on. Veida was having a big pool party. Yancy was acting like he didn't want to go, but he knew that it was the jam of the summer. I had told them all how awesome her house was when she invited Asia, Perlicia, and me to stay over to help get everything ready. After much cleaning and begging, Mom let me go.

"Your mom is stricter than a military sergeant," Veida teased, as the four of us had girl talk in her bonus room.

"No, she just remembered a whole lot of stuff that went on with me and you," I said.

"I'm so glad I didn't have to ask nobody's permission. It ain't like my mom cares where I am," Asia said.

All four of us were broken and had issues with our folks where we thought everything wasn't picture perfect. Though we had been a little jealous of each other during our eighth-grade year, we now had an interesting sisterhood.

"My sister and her girlfriends are always getting into it," Veida said. "Next year she's going to be a senior and hating that I'm going to be on the campus with her."

Veida continued, "I guess I just never had girlfriends I could talk to about stuff. Though I want to be the perfect friend, I always manage to say the wrong thing or do something stupid to make them not care for me anymore." Then she looked at me.

"I'm not trying to sound perfect either," I said. "For the longest time, my brothers and Myrek were my friends, so I know what you're saying. Asia and Perlicia were the ones who had the girlfriend bond. They've been tight for years, looking down on me and stuff. I don't think they even wanted to be my friend until they saw me hanging out with you, Veida."

"Oh see, why you going to throw us out like that?" Asia tried to defend herself.

"I'm just calling a spade a spade. Come on, right? In sixth and seventh grade y'all weren't even trying to be with me," I said.

"That's because you looked like a boy most of the time. You didn't care to fix yourself up. Eighth-grade year, girl, you came in popping, working it. You were taking all the guys. We couldn't beat you, so we had to join you, and make you part of our crew," Perlicia said.

"Y'all have to admit," Asia said, "the four of us are so fly. At this party, we'll have all the heads spinning."

I wasn't down for dissing any other girls and trying to be all up in dudes' faces so they'd notice me. But the bond in the sisterhood that we were forming, as we talked through who we hoped would come to the bash the next day, was extremely exciting.

"I can't believe you got a pool!" Asia said to Veida.

Veida didn't respond to that. She had other things on her mind and said, "I bought four bathing suits. Y'all got to tell me which one is the best."

I was just planning to wear some shorts and a T-shirt. With the fire and everything, my swimsuit from last year was gone. Although it probably wouldn't have fit right anyway, I would've made it work. I wasn't trying to look like a fool. As the three of them modeled their outfits, I sat over in the corner too embarrassed to admit that I didn't have a dime to buy any bathing suit.

"Your body is slamming," Veida said as she came over to me. "Why don't you take this one. I know it would look really cute on you. Ain't even no need in me trying to put it on, girl. I can't work it like you can."

"You don't have to do that," I said to her, knowing that she was taking pity on me.

"Go ahead and try it on," Asia said, with three brand new bathing suits of her own to choose from. Her cousin had hooked her up.

Perlicia had one that was awesome. "It's my mom's. She ain't even going to notice I even wore it. Go ahead and try yours on, Yasmin."

After some more convincing, I stepped into the bathroom. I couldn't believe it myself that I had as many curves as I did. Yeah, I saw myself every day, but I didn't really check myself out. I looked good. When I stepped into my girls' view, they were speechless.

"You'll have everyone staring," Asia finally said.

"Y'all, it's not all that," I said.

"Yeah, girl, you're fitting it, but you're not really feeling it," Perlicia said, as she spun me around.

Veida started talking about who she was expecting to come to her party. "I invited some of the new guys y'all are going to meet next year. And they are cute." I already knew there were going to be some kids from Veida's old middle school going to high school with us. The more she kept talking about these new guys, one of them started to sound familiar.

"Your ex-boyfriend is coming? The one York and I saw you with at the basketball game?" I asked.

"Yeah," Veida responded.

"Why didn't you tell him about my brother? I thought the point was for y'all to get back together," I said.

"She's the ocean," Perlicia said. "More than one fish can swim."

"Not when one of them is my brother and he's a little tadpole swimming with sharks," I said.

"Yasmin, are you saying Yancy and I got a chance again?" Veida asked.

"No, I mean, I don't know—" I couldn't even finish the statement. But it felt like I had set him up. I liked for my family to have all the information before they got thrown into a situation and blindsided.

"Yancy's a big boy. You can tell him in the morning that if he doesn't want to come, he punks out, and he'll just deal with Maurice at school. And the word will get out," Veida said with an attitude.

I got up and walked out of the room. Veida followed me.

"What?" I asked.

"I'm just being real, Yasmin."

"Veida, you can't play two guys against each other, particularly when one of them is my brother and you say that you want to be my friend."

"I thought you got it the last time, Yasmin. Why you gotta keep trying to cause all this drama? It's not like I invited Maurice personally, but I know he's coming because the rest of his boys are.

And I didn't want to keep them from coming because they'd make the night more interesting. I know inside that sweet innocent girl is a big girl ready to come out and meet more people."

Veida walked away and left me to think about all she had said. At that point, it didn't matter how I perceived myself. Was I going to let how she viewed me turn out to be the real me? Or, was I losing my mind in the summer heat? Too many questions; hopefully I could find the right answers.

The only problem with not having a cell phone wasn't just everybody else teasing me; it was that I really couldn't get in touch with people when I needed to. I had to leave Uncle John a message to give to Yancy. But there was no way I could give him too much information, or he'd not let me even go to the party. So, I played greeter at the door. My mom and Mr. Mike dropped off York, Yancy, and Myrek. I threw a towel around me quickly and waved out the door. York flew past me, barely saying hi.

Myrek tried to speak but I said, "I really need to talk to Yancy. It's pretty important. I'll catch up with you down there."

Myrek said okay and started walking toward the pool with some of his basketball teammates.

"What? Sis, what? I'm about to check out the ladies," Yancy playfully protested.

"Boy, please," I said to him.

"What do you want to talk to me about?"

"Yancy, I think Veida is trying to make you jealous."

"Like that's a surprise. She's been trying to get with this for what? Six months?"

"It's the guy from her old school. He'll be going to high school

with us, you know. The one York and I saw her with at the basketball game, they were all hugged up."

"Okay, okay, I get the picture. Whatever. She can be with some
other dude. That isn't going to rattle my cage now," Yancy said.

"It's not going to be that many girls here," I said.

"That's what you think. We invited a ton of them. This party
is 'bout to get crunk," Yancy said, smiling too wide.

"I just don't know those dudes. They might try you and your
boys," I said.

"Well, you know York is crazy. And Myrek is too," Yancy said,
"and I ain't no punk. Don't let the brains fool you."

Just then, somebody blew past him and brushed him hard. He
fell into me and the towel fell off.

"Man, who's the hottie in the bathing suit!?" This guy with a
gold tooth said to a boy who looked kind of familiar.

"Watch it, man," Yancy said to him.

"You watch it," Maurice replied.

"Okay, Yancy, you got to go for real," I said.

"Oh, that's the dude? He can have Veida. I'm through with her
anyway," Yancy said really loud. "You can have my leftovers if you're
even man enough to handle it."

The two of them started tussling. Everybody ran over to where
they were getting into it.

Then the guy with the gold tooth grabbed my arm and said,
"You too fine in that bathing suit." Then he extended his arms for
me to reach out and hug him. Before I knew it, I felt his lips on my
neck. So, with my free hand I punched him in the gut as hard as I
could. As if I was wrestling with York or Yancy.

"Don't act like you don't want to get with Slick Will," the dude said to me as he started backing off.

Then I heard a welcomed voice. "Is he bothering you?" Myrek stepped to us and asked.

"I handled him. Yancy and I both were trying to get folks outta our faces!"

"Can we talk, Yasmin?" Myrek asked.

"Yeah, sure," I said as we started walking away from the crowd.

York pulled Yancy away from Maurice. Asia, Perlicia, and Veida were all on the dance floor having a great time. A whole lot of people were playing in the pool. Myrek walked me over to an empty bench. The food wasn't ready so nobody was sitting down yet.

"Why are you dressed like that?" he asked me.

"Like what?" I asked.

"That swimsuit is too tight," Myrek said.

"It's just a swimsuit. This is a pool party. You're walking around in your swimming trunks."

"But I got on long shorts, to my knees. Don't even compare it. The guys are all over you, and it's sort of like you're asking for it the way you're dressed."

"I didn't ask for anything. That's why I made sure he knew it, and I didn't need your help working that situation out either. I had it under control," I said.

"The dude was getting loud with you and why you gotta make this hard on me? You know I care about you. You know I want to be with you. You don't want to be with me. But then you walk around like this, inviting any ol' guy to see you looking this way," Myrek said.

"Absolutely nothing wrong with guys looking," I said.

"So you want that?"

"No, Myrek, that's not what I'm saying. I'm just saying it's a party. It's summertime, it's hot, and I'm cooling out." Then I noticed both of my brothers standing near me. I knew they would have something to say too.

"Dudes are talking about you all over the party! You need to put on some clothes," York said, as he threw a towel in my face.

Yancy picked up on it. "Yeah, because I don't want to get to fighting up in here over my ex-girl and my sister. These dudes from West Middle School are crazy."

Myrek walked off and I followed him, ignoring both my brothers. They didn't need to act all protective or anything. I knew how to handle myself. What I didn't know how to deal with was my feelings for Myrek. Being in this bathing suit and getting a lot of looks felt a little uncomfortable but not so much that I wanted to run and hide. Seeing him acting jealous tugged at my heart. I touched his shoulder and we stopped under the moonlight.

"Do what you want to do, Yasmin. I can't make—" Before he could finish his sentence, I planted a kiss on his lips. He pulled my body to his and I liked the closeness we felt. I knew if my Uncle John saw me, he'd kill me. If my mom could see me, she definitely wouldn't approve. But, somehow that didn't stop what I was feeling.

"Okay, wait. Where'd that come from?" Myrek said when the kiss was done.

"They say the summer heat makes you lose your mind," I said.

"Is this for real?" he asked.

I said, giggling, "Just as real as summer is here."

Chapter Five

Ponder
the Thought

"So, does this mean you're my girlfriend?" Myrek said as he pulled away from my lips.

I was so astonished. I couldn't believe I had kissed him. What was I doing? This was so wrong. My knees started to shake, my heart started to race, and I just wanted to be left alone. Myrek's eyes widened. I could tell he knew I was completely uncomfortable and wanted to take back our actions. And when he reached out for me, I ran in the opposite direction as fast and as far as I could.

When I got into the woods, I didn't even realize how scary it was until I heard all kinds of noises from critters that frightened me. I'd been away from the party for about twenty minutes, so I knew people would worry. Even with that I couldn't go back. I felt so ashamed because a part of me liked it.

There's a connection that Myrek and I had that was deeper than ever before. Now he was talking about me being his girlfriend. What was that about? What came after kissing? What would he expect? Pondering all the things that could transpire, and when I saw myself pregnant like his sister Jada, I knew I wanted no part in any of that. I prayed.

Lord, I'm sorry it seems like I let You down. Myrek was right, I'm parading around trying to get guys to look at me. Trying to be cute for what, to bring trouble to myself? And then a guy that I do like, I'm sending him mixed signals because I'm all mixed up. Is it wrong for me to like him? Or, am I just trying to give him what he wants because I don't want him to be with anybody else? What does that say about me as a person? I know I'm young and I know I'm not going to get it all right. My mom even told me that. I'm smart, I know how to make good choices, or at least I thought I did till now. I need Your help to stay on the right course. I want to be happy and experience true joy, but I know I'm messing up. Help me, please. Amen.

When I tried to go back to Veida's house, I got lost. I could no longer hear the loud party music or the kids screaming from having a great time. Where had I wondered off to, and how in the world would I get back?

All of a sudden, a wild dog came upon me with sharp teeth and a salivating mouth. I was petrified. As he inched closer I knew that I couldn't freak out or I'd be through. Before I could do anything, the dog charged at me. Suddenly, there was Myrek with a big stick chasing the dog away. Again I found myself in his arms, thanking him for being there.

He wanted to take it further. He wanted us to be a couple. How could I tell him that wasn't what I was up for? How could I let him know that's not what I wanted? I didn't want to break his heart. I'd been down this road with him before. I didn't want to make him mad. I mean, he had just saved me, for goodness' sake. But, I had to be honest.

"Why'd you run away?" he asked. "Yasmin, I want to protect you. I want to take care of you. You don't have to be scared of what you're feeling."

He stepped closer to me. Because suddenly a big chill came blowing in the night's air, I appreciated his body shielding me from the breeze. Then he kissed my cheek. I twinkled inside just like the stars above.

"No, you don't understand," I tried to tell him as I stayed in place, letting my actions send a different signal.

"I can't. This isn't right. But, I know how I feel about you. I think about you all the time. Like in the morning when I wake up and at night when I go to sleep," I said.

Then a bunch of lights shined on us. I was so startled, I didn't realize what was happening.

"I can't believe this, Yasmin Peace! I let you go to a party and here I find you in the woods with some boy," my mom yelled out. There she was with Mr. Mike and a gang of people behind her.

She walked over and slapped me hard.

"Miss Peace, this isn't her fault," Myrek tried to explain.

"Oh, I know she's not in it alone. Trust me. I just hope I caught you two before . . . Ugh! Yasmin, I can't even tell you how disappointed I am. And, what the rest of y'all looking at?" my mom said to about thirty kids who were supposed to be in Veida's backyard.

Tears started streaming down my face. My mom had gotten the wrong idea. Or, was she dead right? Did I need this kind of wake-up call?

"Thanks a lot," Veida came over and angrily said to me. "Because you went missing, my dad's shutting down the party."

"What do you mean, missing?" I asked.

"Yasmin, everyone's been looking for you," Veida said.

"Man, sis, I'm glad you're all right," York said.

"I just got out of the hospital. Mom wouldn't be able to take it if you were in one."

"Let's go, Yasmin!" Mom yelled at me.

"Go ahead, join your son and take us home," Mom said, fussing at Mr. Mike.

"Please, Miss Peace. Seriously, it was my fault," Myrek said.

"Son, just let it go. You know you aren't supposed to be out here with her like this," Mr. Mike scolded.

"I just went looking for her, Dad," Myrek explained.

"Yeah, and we find you guys alone out here. Come on, Son, I wasn't born yesterday. I know you like the girl, but you don't want to get yourself into something you can't handle," Mr. Mike said sternly.

I couldn't believe they were talking about me like that, as if I was nowhere around. I was completely humiliated and tried to dash off in front of everyone, but my mother jerked my hand back so I had to walk with her.

Asia came up on the other side of me and said, "I know how you must be feeling, but look at how many people care. We were searching for you, girl. I was hoping to find you because I knew Myrek went looking for you. But this could have been worse. At least you're all right."

"Ugh, you think I'm all right. My mom slapped me. Everybody saw it. I'll probably be grounded for a month, and I didn't want to be with him like that."

"Girl, please. Go and tell that to somebody else. We saw y'all."
I sighed.

⁓

"I don't understand why I have to go to Big Mama's house. It's like you are so disappointed in me that you're sending me away," I said. My mom was driving me down to Orlando to spend a few weeks with my grandma.

"Well, it's crowded at your Uncle John's house, and we won't be able to move out for a couple of weeks. They're complaining about their water bill, electric bill, and all their stuff. Your brothers are going to basketball camp. This gets you out of the house for a while, and maybe Big Mama can talk some sense into you. You're a little bit faster than I thought you were."

"Mom, you misunderstood everything you saw the other night."

"Well, my mind keeps racing, Yasmin. And the stuff that I'm thinking about my baby girl doing is stuff you ain't ready for. I need to get you far away from Myrek."

I had no idea what I was going to do at Big Mama's house. I loved her and all, but this just felt like punishment. My house had already been taken away. It wasn't like I ever owned a cell phone or even a landline for that matter. I couldn't even remember the last time I had new clothes. I didn't know why Mom wanted to separate me from her and my brothers. Aunt Lucinda had found a job and I was even going to be helping with the baby. I just didn't understand.

"Yasmin, don't sit over there rolling your eyes. You think it's okay that everybody was at some party that I let you go to, and then I catch you in the woods with a boy, about to do who knows what. Now, I've known Myrek most of his life. He's a good kid, but you guys are teenagers. That little tom girl Yasmin, who used to climb trees with him, is no more."

All of a sudden she popped me on my head after we had been driving in silence for fifteen minutes.

"Oww!!!" I screamed.

"I just don't understand you, Yasmin. What were you thinking, girl? Have we gotten away from where you feel like you can tell me anything? One minute you like him, the next minute you guys ain't speaking. Is it my dating his dad that is planting seeds in your head? Everything you see, baby, is not as good as it looks."

"I don't know, Ma."

"Speak up. I can't hear you mumbling."

"It just sort of happened," I said.

"Being in compromising situations with young men just don't happen, girl."

"You know he's liked me for a while, Ma. We even fell out because of it. I don't know, it's like I went to bed and woke up the next day and I was interested in boys. But, not just *any* boy; it's a boy who's been there all along. A boy who I know really cares about me. I wasn't trying to go all the way with him or anything, and I didn't mean to embarrass you or nothing like that. I was in the woods because I ran away from him."

"I don't understand," Mom said.

"That's what I am trying to tell you, if you would let me talk," I said.

"Listen, don't get smart with me, Miss Lady."

"I'm just saying, Ma. I kissed him. Then I hated myself for it. I tried to get as far away from him as I could. Before I knew it, I was in some woods. I was further away from the house than I thought. A wild, crazy dog was about to attack me and, out of nowhere, there was Myrek to save the day. That's how I ended up in his arms again. That's pretty much what everybody saw. I know he thinks I'm absolutely crazy. Leading him on and then completely turning it off."

"Well, you don't need to be worried about what he thinks right now. You don't need to be alone at no time soon. The only time I plan for you to see that boy is on the school bus—with fifty other kids."

"So, you're shipping me off to Big Mama's and locking me in my room when I get back. What's that going to do?" I asked.

She leaned back and put her head against the headrest. I waited for her to answer but her eyes watered up instead. Her hands started shaking on the steering wheel and she got off on the next exit. We didn't need any gas but she stopped at a station anyway.

She looked me dead in my eyes and said, "If you end up like me, I'd be heartbroken."

"Ma, you're a great mother."

"Yes, but I had Jeff Jr. way too young. And even with him havin' a lot on the ball, he was about to follow my same pattern with Jada. I know I'm busy working my job. Yeah, I'm hanging out a little with Mr. Mike. But, I don't want you to think that I don't love you."

"I know you do, Ma. I just need a little room to breathe. You gotta trust me to make some mistakes too."

"But that's just it, baby. Some mistakes will mess you up and ruin your life, and because I been there and done that, I'm not going to allow you to run in those quicksand shoes. Promise me, baby, that you're gonna keep your head on straight, that you'll leave the boys alone. Trust me, you'll have time for that. Stay focused. Give yourself more opportunities. Plan to go to college. Maybe even get one of those higher degrees. A masters, a doctorate, or something. You are so smart."

"Ma, I am not smart."

"You count yourself short. Every time you apply yourself you get it done. You might not be in them advanced classes like Yancy, but so what. That doesn't mean you're not smart. You're just a little lazy that's all. I just want you to be down here and help Big Mama out. Your Aunt Yolanda said she's been talking crazy sometimes and sort of seeing things. You being down here will help us out. I know this feels like a punishment, but it's not."

Mom kept on talking. I could tell from her tone that she was really concerned about me and my future. "Just take this time and think about you. Think about what you really want to become and think about the choices and the things that you've been doing now. It will affect your future. I believe if you really dig deep and have some quiet time with God, you're gonna come back ready for high school. You got to be in the right mind-set, Yasmin. And what I saw the other day in the woods with that little boy was just not the Yasmin that I know."

I looked up to the sky. She started up the car and we drove on to Big Mama's. Maybe a few weeks away from all the craziness in my little world would help me gain perspective.

⤜❧⤏

"Hey there, baby," my grandma said as soon as she saw me. She squeezed my cheeks really hard. She squeezed me so tight. I knew she loved me and was happy to see me, but I could hardly breathe.

I gave my mom a look like, *Uh huh, why are you doing this to me? Maybe I don't want to stay down here.*

But she replied, "Oh, Mom, Yasmin is so excited to come spend time with you for a couple of weeks."

I just shook my head. She got me. The two of them talked for a while and my aunt came over with her daughter Alyssa.

"What's up, cuz?" My cousin had on all the latest gear.

Alyssa was going to the tenth grade, and she and I hadn't really kept in touch that much. We did have a lot in common, though. Not only were our moms sisters, but we both had dads that didn't live with us. Her brother, Kyle, was a year younger than me, and though her mom had a job, they didn't have money like Veida's family.

"What's up, girl? I got something to show you. I'm so glad you're here. We can get paid this summer."

"Paid! A job! What?"

As quickly as I wanted to leave, now she was talking about getting paid big bucks. That changed my mind and all of a sudden I was excited to stay. She pulled me to the back room where I would be staying, opened up a laptop, and pulled up a Web site. It was taking a few minutes to load.

"You got wireless?" I said to her.

"Yeah, my mom thinks I'm always on here doing papers, research, and stuff. Girl, I'm fooling her. I'm just having some fun."

"Alyssa, come here. Your aunt wants to see you," Aunt Yolanda said.

"Okay, click on 'high school loot' as soon as it opens. I'll be right back. If my mom comes in here, close the window."

And then Alyssa was gone. What was she thinking I could make money doing? My eyes got larger than they ever had before when I saw electronics being sold for less than half their real value. What was Alyssa into, and why would she think I would want to be in it with her? This was a hot mess. The site advertised stolen goods. "You don't tell, we won't tell!"

When she came back she asked, "You down? All we got to do is deliver the stuff. This guy said I could make $500. And if I knew somebody else I could get a referral fee. You'll get paid $500 too. Let's make some money. It's no big deal. We didn't steal nothing."

She went over to the computer and opened it up again. I couldn't believe how exited she was about being a part of something criminal. I knew dollars were tight, but I wasn't trying to get paid by any means necessary.

"Girl, what y'all doing in here?" Mom said as I jumped when she startled us and opened the door.

"Nothing, Ma," I said.

"Nothing much, Auntie. I'm just showing her some of the research that helped me with my papers at school. You know, high school is a little tougher than middle school so I'm trying to school her early," Alyssa said, lying through her teeth. I guess I was doing the same thing since I told my mother nothing was going on. But how could I say anything right then?

"You are in such good hands, Yasmin. I told you Alyssa was going to be great for you. Be good and y'all take care of your grandma," my mom said as she left out of the room.

Pulling me before I could follow Alyssa said, "I'm glad you're out here because I'm tired of staying with Big Mama. She's off the chain now, having tea parties with rabbits and all kinds of crazy stuff."

I didn't know whether to believe Alyssa or not, so I left out of the room and I asked Mom about it and she said that Big Mama had been sort of forgetful lately. She's started wandering away from home, but my mom and Aunt Yolanda were watching the situation closely. She said it was good that I could be there at Big Mama's house with Aunt Yolanda and my cousins to help out. She said if Big Mama didn't improve, she and Aunt Yolanda were gonna have to have a long talk about what to do.

I walked my mother to the car and she kept going on and on about how great Alyssa was. *If she only knew*, I thought. But, it wasn't my place to rat my cousin out. I did have to be in Orlando with Alyssa a couple of weeks, but I knew the adventure she was trying to get me to partake in would only lead to more trouble.

My mom thought me spending time with Big Mama and my family down here was a good idea. I hoped she was right. I kissed her good-bye and felt really sad when she left.

It wasn't long before night fell, and I kept thinking back to when I was in the woods with Myrek. I was being honest with myself, very truthful about the whole thing. I didn't hate being with him. I just hated that I liked it so much. But what was I supposed to do with all those feelings? I mean, I was just about to turn fourteen and, as my mom said, I needed to stay focused and stay on the right track. She told me to make sure I got everything right, not wrong.

But I couldn't dismiss what I was feeling. I had to find a way to deal with it, conquer it, and reach out to Myrek. When he and I started high school we needed to be on one accord, but I wasn't ready to do that just yet.

Big Mama woke me up. I looked at the clock and it was midnight. She asked me if I heard that band in the backyard. There was dead silence. No band, no nothing. I didn't know what she was talking about. I was so sleepy that I just drifted off to sleep.

I remember that I couldn't get comfortable and my throat got scratchy. So, about two in the morning I woke up. When I passed by her room, the door was open. I just wanted to peep in and make sure she was okay. I mean, my grandma had taken care of me for so long, loving me, praying for me, and all that good stuff. But she wasn't in her bed. I looked in the kitchen and she wasn't in there. I checked the living room. No sign of her there either.

I started to panic. Where was my grandmother? She was gone and it was the middle of the night. *Had somebody taken her? Had she hurt herself and I slept through it? What in the world was going on?* Too many awful thoughts were going through my mind. I stood there frozen, trying to figure out what to do and praying that everything was okay. All I could do was ponder the thought.

Chapter 6

Disaster
Strikes Again

*A*lyssa, Alyssa, you gotta help!" I said to my cousin. "Big Mama is not in her bed! She's missing! She's gone. I don't know if somebody came and got her. I don't know where she is!" I exclaimed, franctic with worry.

"Ma!" Alyssa screamed out, calling for my aunt. "Big Mama did it again!"

My aunt and cousins lived two blocks away, but they had been staying with Big Mama since the family was concerned about her health.

Aunt Yolanda shouted, "Oh, no! I just checked on her not too long ago and she was asleep!" as she went from room to room searching.

Alyssa called 911, and Aunt Yolanda began looking outside. She started drilling me with questions: How long had I been up? When did I notice her missing? I just started to cry and my aunt couldn't get any more answers out of me.

Just hearing sirens coming actually made me have chest pains. It reminded me of the sirens that I heard the day we found Jeff shot, or the sirens that sounded when York was caught in the fire. Each time the sirens came because of such bad news.

The sheriff started to ask a million questions: How long had she been missing? Where did we look for her? Did she do anything else strange that night? I just wanted this to stop and all of this to be a bad dream, but it wasn't. What was going on with my grandma? And if I was really supposed to watch her closely because she had taken off and disappeared before, why hadn't somebody explained that to me? Because if I would have known, I would have done a better job of looking out for her.

My grandmother's neighbor, Miss Alberta, came out and said to me, "I know you're scared. They gonna find her, though. She's gonna be all right."

I just looked up at the dark sky and prayed, *Lord, help us find her.* My aunt said that Big Mama was behaving like someone who had Alzheimer's and that she was scheduled to go to the doctor this week. What was going on? I didn't know much about the disease. I just knew it was something that made people forget stuff.

Then, walking toward me in the distance, it looked like the silhouette of Big Mama. I started running, and when I got to her I threw my arms around her. She was in one piece and she had just been taking a stroll.

"Big Mama, you scared me. Oh, my gosh, are you okay?"

"Who are you?" she responded. "Get off of me. Help! Help!" she screamed.

"Big Mama, it's me. It's Yasmin. Yvette's daughter. Tell me you know who I am." She wouldn't let me calm her down. She just wanted to get away from me. The two rescue workers and police-men came running over to us.

"Why are y'all trying to get me?" she screamed.

Aunt Yolanda went over to her and tried to comfort my grand-mother. When she had finally calmed her down, she said to the officers, "I can't do this anymore. This is just too hard. This is the second time she ran away this month. Something's going on and my mother might hurt herself."

My aunt then started filling out some paperwork that one of the policemen gave her. Alyssa and her brother, Kyle, came over to me.

"Hey, cuz. This is deep and sad, ain't it?" Kyle asked.

"Yeah, I mean, she didn't even know me," I answered him. "This is weird. Your mom said Big Mama might have Alzheimer's. I don't understand it. Is she gonna know herself in a few minutes? My mom already told me that Big Mama was forgetting things lately and that she'd wandered off."

Looking extremely bummed out, Kyle said, "Big Mama's been getting worse."

"Well, my mom was hoping that would not be the case. Before she left she told me that if Big Mama did get worse then she and your mom would have to do something more," I said.

"Good because I don't want see her suffer," Kyle said.

All of a sudden, my grandmother started putting up even more of a fuss as the two men in uniform were trying to get her on the stretcher. As if she sensed that I wanted to help, she called out, "Yasmin, don't let them take me!"

I ran over to her again and this time I held her as tight as I could. I didn't want her to go, I just wanted her to be the way she always had been—full of love and care for her family.

My aunt said, "Sweetheart, you don't understand. Big Mama is sick. You just don't know how hard this has been."

"But I wanna go back to my house," Big Mama cried.

"But, Ma, you just ran away. We have to take you to the hospital to get you checked out," Aunt Yolanda explained to her in a sweet voice.

Aunt Yolanda got into the ambulance with my grandmother, and my aunt's friend Miss Alberta stayed with us overnight. It almost broke my heart, but it certainly would have been worse if she had gotten hurt. *Maybe she needed help that Mom and Aunt Yolanda can't provide for her,* I thought, as I went back inside to the place I'd always known as comforting.

There had been many good family times in Big Mama's house. Over the years, we've shared delicious food, had lots of fun with my cousins and other family members, and listened to Big Mama telling stories about what it was like to live in the old days.

The next morning when my aunt came back from the hospital, she explained to us that Big Mama might have to go to a nursing home.

I said to her, "But, Aunt Yolanda, I just don't understand why Big Mama has to go to a nursing home."

"That's right, baby," she answered me, "you simply don't understand. You just came down here. You and your mama have your own set of problems. I know what's best here and though it may seem cruel in your eyes, I'm not going to harm my own mother. This is what's best for her. Trust me. I know."

"I want to call my mom," I said, feeling sick all over.

Aunt Yolanda had clearly made a decision. "Well, baby, your

mom and I talked last night. But Yvette was uneasy with it at first, but the more we talked the more she understood that I had to do what I had to do. Putting Big Mama in a nursing home is the only way to handle this because she can't live on her own any longer. Even though she could live with us, I have to go to work, so no one would be here to care for her. This is what's best for her. You can call your mom and talk about it. But Yasmin honestly I ain't been feeling good myself since all this started months back. It might not seem like it, but this is best for everyone."

I ran to the back room. If my mom already knew, I didn't need to talk to her about it. I was mad at the world. My grandma was such a strong and special lady. She already didn't live the high life. Why did she have to have such a low disease? I always appreciated the wise things she said and now that was taken from her too. It just really killed me. But, what could I do but pray?

⋙

A week later, I was so angry when I woke up. It was my birthday. I was away from my family. My mom thought she was going to be able to come and pick me up, but something had happened on her job and she wasn't able to get off. All I wanted to do was go home. Aunt Yolanda wasn't treating me badly, but there was a little tension because she knew that I didn't agree with her sending my grandma away. And, as if it couldn't be worse, I couldn't even go and see her. Since the doctors were trying to get Big Mama to adjust to her new surroundings in the nursing home, the rest of us weren't able to visit her, only my aunt.

I was beginning to see how Alyssa was wild in a lot more ways than me. Every day when her mom left for work or went to visit

Big Mama, my cousin was into something mischievous. We had already gotten into it a couple of times because I told her that I was not going to lie for her.

"Okay, Yasmin, I know it's your birthday, and I know we haven't been getting along. But look, let's just enjoy the day," she said as she came over and gave me a great big hug.

I knew her too well. I knew that she wanted something, so I didn't even smile. She was up to something.

"Come on, loosen up. You gotta believe me. I really want to get along with you," she tried to convince me.

Her brother had gone to spend some time with his father. They had different dads, and Kyle's dad lived in Miami.

"It's just the two of us. We can enjoy your birthday, or we can ignore each other. What do you want to do? If you could choose anything in the world that you wanted to happen, what would you want to do today?" Alyssa asked.

"I want to talk to my mom and my brothers."

"Well, you can call them. See, I got three cell phones. Take your pick," Alyssa said.

She showed me the cutest cell phones. I couldn't help but smile.

"Now, you can't have one, but you can definitely use it all day. Here, call anybody you want."

"Thanks," I said as I reached out and gave her a big hug.

"Now, what else do you want?"

"I'd love to go and see my dad."

She squinted her eyes for a minute as if she was thinking about it. Then she pulled out her phone and sent out a couple of texts.

"Okay, we can catch the bus over there. I think visiting hours are from ten to three."

As we waited for the bus to arrive, I called Uncle John's house and Aunt Lucinda answered. "Yasmin, girl, we miss you. Angel is getting so big. Your mom said you'd be home next week. Can't wait to see you, girl. I'm the only one here right now, so I'll have to give them your message. Happy birthday, big fourteen-year-old!"

I hated to admit it, but I was a little bummed. My brothers were doing something cool without me. We always celebrated our birthday together. But Mom made me come here and that really hurt. I looked at the phone as if staring at it would make it ring.

I pondered the thought of calling Myrek. I didn't know if he would be in or not. I hadn't spoken to him since I'd left. But I couldn't bring myself to call him. I looked at the phone but couldn't even enter his number. I didn't want to start something that I wasn't sure would even work.

We took a couple of buses to get to the jail, and Alyssa was nice by letting me listen to her iPod. After my visit with Dad, we were planning to go and get my hair hooked up. That's how I thought cousins were supposed to act, but since it hadn't been this way I really didn't know what she wanted.

When we got off the bus, I looked at the big jailhouse. I had visited it once before with my mom and brothers around Thanksgiving time. As we started walking toward the building, my knees started to buckle. I really did want to see my dad. I needed him to say that he loved me, but I was feeling intimidated by my surroundings.

"What's wrong?" Alyssa said, as we reached the huge iron gate.

"I should let him know that I'm coming and make sure my mom is even cool with me being here," I told her.

"Your mom? This is your birthday girl. Your mom would want

you to enjoy it. Plus, as long as her sister's cool with whatever you're doing, she's fine. And my mom always says y'all should see your dad more It's all good. Come on. Mr. Smith is waiting on us."

"Who is Mr. Smith?" I asked.

"Well, we can't get in there without an adult because we're not eighteen, so I called my friend."

"Oh, no. No, you didn't have to do that," I said, uneasy about meeting a stranger.

Then her phone went off. I guess it was a text. She looked at it and said, "He's already inside and they already got your dad waiting. Let's go."

At first, my feet did not move. I was so reluctant. Alyssa looked at me till I complied. She talked to Mr. Smith. I went with the officer to see my father. Finally, I was alone in a room with my father. He stood to his feet and I rushed to hug him. Being in his arms made the way I got here worth it.

"How's my baby? Pretty soon, birthday girl, you won't have to visit me here."

"Oh Daddy, I hope so. I miss you."

"I miss you too. I miss you all. I mean, every time something big has happened with our family, I wasn't around to help. Now, your brother caught in a fire. You know York's my heart. He trying to be a hero, gonna get himself killed."

"I know, Daddy. It was so scary."

"I'm sure, baby girl. But, I'm proud of you guys for helping your neighbor."

"I didn't do anything."

"Yeah, you did, you called 911. I talked to Uncle John. He also told me why your mom sent you down here for a few weeks."

"These weeks have seemed more like an eternity," I said.

"So, you think you can kiss a boy now, and get all involved in all that?"

It was so cool talking to Dad because he wasn't ridiculing me or going off. That was typically Mom's style. I was surprised, though, when he took my hand and said, "I talked to you before about the choices I made that got me in here. You're fourteen today, baby girl. You're growing up. You got a bright future ahead of you. Don't get involved in anything serious right now. Who is he, anyway?"

"He's a good guy, Daddy. He really is. You'd like him. He's been friends with all three of us for so long. But, all of a sudden I just think about him as more than just a friend. I can't explain it. I want to shake those feelings away—I really do."

"Well, sweetheart," he said as he leaned over and kissed my forehead. "Dad hasn't been around to give you advice and to tell you how special you are. You don't need a young man in your life that can't wait on you. If you're feeling pressure and this dude is getting upset, then you need to cut ties. Maybe it's best not to even be friends right now. It would be better to not have him in your life and you remain okay, instead of you letting him be a part of it and something horrible happens. Be smart for me, okay?"

I was so happy he didn't ask me who brought me to see him and I didn't say nothing. I knew he thought it was my aunt. I reached out and hugged him. It felt so great to have a dad. That was a great present.

As soon as I came out, Alyssa and Mr. Smith were waiting on me. She introduced us and standing before me was a very nice-looking man. He held a grin on his face that would not leave. What did he want, I wondered?

"So, Alyssa told me you guys got a lot of things planned for your birthday. I was going to drive you over to the hairdresser and also get your nails and toes done. Is that all right?"

"Oh, you don't have to do all that," I said.

"No, it's okay. I insist," he said. "This is her gift to you."

When we parked in front of the beauty shop, I wanted to go back to my aunt's house. I was too smart to fall for something dumb and this Mr. Smith was being too nice. I just needed to stay alert in the situation. At the same time, it felt so good when I was getting my hair washed. And I so enjoyed getting my nails and toes all pretty. I liked being pampered for my birthday.

Before we went home, Alyssa said Mr. Smith was going to take us to get something to eat. This had been a full day so I agreed. I was pretty hungry.

I watched their actions and he was just a little too playful with her. When he went to the restroom I leaned over and said, "Cuz, how old is he?"

"He's twenty-five," she said, smiling.

"He's ten years older than you, girl."

"I know. That's the man who has the site on the Internet 'Buy Some Loot.' He can hook us up, girl. He's got money and he wants us to steal some stuff for him and shave off the numbers of the products he has at his crib."

"You said what?!" I was shocked.

"Come on, you owe me, Yasmin. You used my phone. I let you wear some of my clothes. He even helped you out by giving you a chance to see your dad. He wouldn't have done that if you hadn't signed up. That's why I did it for you. He paid for your hair and nails and all of that. Now, he's feeding you. Unless you got money to pay him back, you got to work it off. It's no big deal."

When Mr. Smith got back to the table, Alyssa nodded at him. He smiled at me and started going on and on about how much I was going to enjoy making money. I knew she was being nice for some reason. Now she was pulling me into her craziness.

The more I thought about it, I didn't know what to do. I had seen York get in trouble with the law for stealing. I wasn't going to do that. Shucks, Alyssa had boxed me in, and I didn't have a dime to my name. How could I pay this man back for all that he had already shelled out and have a few extra dollars in my pocket to take back home with me? This was a problem, but I kept my cool as I tried to figure out exactly what to do.

When we got to the apartment, it was so nice. It was completely on the other side of the tracks. The place was decked out with the latest equipment and technology; he had four computers stretched out in a row. He had the latest grooves playing and he asked me to go grab the filer and saw off numbers on some flat screen tvs. I went to the drawer he pointed to and stalled. I didn't want to be a part of this.

My cousin, however, had no problem with it. She bumped me out of the way and took out the filer. She went over to the box and zipped through his request.

When she moved to the next box she asked, "You helping?"

"I'm sorry, I can't do this." I had made up my mind and nothing was going to change it.

"Come on, Yasmin. You owe me. You said you were gonna do it."

"I can't," I said as tears welled up in my eyes. Shedding some tears seemed like the best way out.

"I want to go back to your house, Alyssa."

"Here's some money for a cab," he said. "I'll have one here for you in ten minutes. Take my card in case you change your mind. I've got another shipment arriving soon. You know where to find us."

"I can't believe you're doing this," Alyssa said, looking at me. She was furious.

"You're fourteen today," she went on. "Why are you acting like a baby? That's $500 down the drain. Now, I'm going to have to pay for your hair. I'm gonna have to pay for your nails."

"Well, consider it a birthday gift," I said.

"Huh, please. It's not like you got me one last month."

"All right. Well, I'll owe you. I'll pay you back."

There was no reasoning with Alyssa. She was just ticked. As soon as the cab pulled up, I left. I wasn't going to be part of any shady stuff.

An hour later I was back at my aunt's house. When I walked through the door, Aunt Yolanda came from the kitchen and asked, "And where have you been? Where's Alyssa?"

"We . . . we didn't think you'd be home this soon. I don't . . . I . . ."

I couldn't even lie. I couldn't put the sentences together. Nothing came together. Nothing made sense so I just sat down.

"Where is Alyssa?!" she insisted.

"Working," was all I could think to say.

"Working? That girl doesn't have a job."

Aunt Yolanda was drilling me, and I was just tired of the whole thing. I was older now and couldn't cover for her any longer. So I said, "Aunt Yolanda I'm not trying to be disrespectful, but . . ."

"Yasmin you know you can talk to me, say what you have to say."

Reluctantly I continued, "It's just if you don't give her money to buy all those new clothes and all this new stuff she has, where do you think she gets it from? What do you think she's doing to get it? I mean, she doesn't hide any of it from you. You're in charge. You know what's best."

"I know she doesn't have a job. So tell me what she's doing." My aunt sounded very concerned.

I got up and walked away. She came and tugged on my arm and turned me around. She demanded, "You take me to her right now!"

I handed her Mr. Smith's business card. I knew it was all going to hit the fan, but in reality Mr. Smith and Alyssa didn't need to be together despite how much she thought she was safe. He was a crook.

I wasn't expecting my aunt to drag me in the car with her, but she did. When we got there she banged on the door. Nobody answered.

"You say hello." She nudged me.

"Hey, it's me," I said, trying to sound casual.

Mr. Smith opened up the door quickly. "I thought you'd come back," he said. "Good. Alyssa and I just got back from the electronics store. She couldn't steal much cause I felt the clerk was suspicous. No one knows you. I need those iPhones. I've got a buyer needing ten tonight. Let's go."

"She ain't going nowhere with you," my aunt said, pushing the door really hard. There was Alyssa removing three iPhones from her pockets.

My aunt clutched her heart. She didn't speak. Alyssa dropped the stolen merchandise, then she ran over to her mother. I couldn't believe this was happening. Was my aunt okay? No, no she wasn't. She fell to the floor—out cold. I couldn't take this. Disaster strikes again.

Chapter 7

Defender of Truth

*T*his isn't my fault, Alyssa!" I shouted through my tears as my cousin leaned over her mom's body.

She looked back and shouted, "Yes, it is! If you would've stayed out of my business and let me do what I was doing, this wouldn't have happened. You could've helped me raise some money so I could take some of the stress off my mom. Then she wouldn't be here lying on the floor right now. I hate you, Yasmin!"

Those strong words made me hate myself. Was all of this really my fault? Though I wanted to take up for myself, was that even possible? How could I justify my actions? If I hadn't brought my aunt over here, she wouldn't have known that Alyssa was involved in illegal activity. My heart sank to my feet.

"Aw, man I can't get busted. Shoot, I'm on parole," Mr. Smith confessed before he grabbed his keys and dashed out the door.

Frustrated and sad I dialed 911 then silently prayed, *"Lord, I just don't understand. I love You and I'm trying to do right, but everywhere I*

go and everywhere I turn, it seems like everyone I love is going through
something that's life threatening. I feel so worthless. Even when I do the
right thing, I'm not smart enough to keep my nose out of places where it
just doesn't belong. Fix this, Lord. Fix the mess I've made, and I prom-
ise I'll go to my room, to a shell somewhere. I won't come out, I won't talk
to anybody, I won't mess with anybody, I won't do anything. Just help
me, please. Help my aunt. Amen.

It wasn't long before the ambulance came and the rescue workers were able to revive her. Alyssa shot me looks that were so eerie.
I knew she didn't want me anywhere around but I could not leave.
I couldn't go anywhere. Not only did I not have any other place to
go, but I had to make sure my aunt was going to be okay.

Contrary to whatever Alyssa thought, I cared. I didn't mean
for any of this to happen and I wasn't going to go away until I knew
it was all good. When Alyssa got up and went into another room
I followed her. I had never seen my tough cousin sob so badly.

"She's going to be okay," I said to her.

"Yeah, but I'm blaming you. Though I know my mom catch-
ing me stealing was too much for her. You're such a good girl. I
shouldn't have involved you in this."

What was Alyssa saying? Was she all of a sudden taking it back
that I had done this to my aunt? Was she really now owning up to
her part in all of this? Was God trying to tell me that I did do the
right thing by revealing what was going on?

"I'm so angry at you for bringing her over here, Yasmin. I am,
but I'm even madder at myself. My mom didn't want me involved
in crime. I know that hurt her heart. We do struggle, it's hard. She
hates dealing with my daddy and my brother's dad, but she's been
making it," Alyssa said. "I just want more. I'm never satisfied. I want

the easy way out, but maybe this is my wake-up call. Maybe I don't need to do this. I want my mom to be okay, Yasmin, but I know she's going to kill me."

"Your mom loves you, Alyssa," I said as I went over and stroked my cousin's hair.

"Be strong. We got to go to the hospital."

Before the ambulance pulled off, a police car drove up. We gave the officers a description of Mr. Smith's car. He was going to have his own trouble for having a house full of stolen goods and selling them.

Both of us were shaking as we rode in the ambulance with my aunt. She had to be okay. That was the only thing that mattered at that moment.

⚜

The next morning Miss Alberta brought us all back to Aunt Yolanda's place. Thankfully, even though she was diagnosed with having a mild heart attack, she was okay but she had to rest in bed. After Alyssa and I got her settled, I called my mom and she said she would immediately be on her way to see about Big Mama and Aunt Yolanda and to get me.

I thought Alyssa and I had straightened everything out. I mean, she admitted she had no business doing what she was doing but she was bitter again.

"If you would've just kept your nose out of it, Yasmin. My friend just called. They caught Mr. Smith. Now, he's going to jail. He was trying to help me. He would've helped you."

"But he's not supposed to steal. There are reasons we have laws and if you break them then you have to pay the consequences."

"Yeah, you would know with a dad in jail most of your life."

Ugh, I couldn't believe she said that to me. It hurt so badly that I didn't have my dad with me every day, but she didn't either. And her dad had no excuse; he was just a deadbeat nobody.

So I lashed out and said, "Better to have one in jail instead of having one walking the streets not wanting to be a part of my life at all. At least my dad loves me. He would be with me if he could. What you got to say for yours?"

Alyssa and I were saying things to each other that we couldn't take back, but we were both being totally honest.

It was a brutal argument until we heard her mom call out, "Girls, come here!"

Our intention was to allow her mom to sleep and get her rest.

"Yeah, Mom, sorry we woke you," Alyssa said.

Aunt Yolanda laid it all out. "I just don't understand you girls. You both have had it hard. I'm lying here trying to rest, and I hear you guys attacking each other over the unfortunate circumstances in both your lives. You all are cousins and, Alyssa, if you're mad at Yasmin for telling me where you were, then you need to check yourself. That man had no business having you over to his apartment. Me and you got some serious talking to do about why you felt stealing for any reason was okay."

Then she turned to me. "And, Yasmin, if you're beating yourself up and thinking that you were wrong to take me over there and that you caused me to have a slight heart attack, then you're wrong. I've been worried about so much, I have high blood pressure, and I didn't pass the stress test I took last month. What's going on with me is my own fault, but I did pull through. If there's ever a time to rejoice about something good, it's now. We can't dwell on what happened or why, or any of that, but we can certainly be thankful."

⋙⟐⋘

"I'm so proud of you, Yasmin," my mother said, placing her arms around me. It was late in the evening when she arrived at her sister's place.

I had been in such a funk. Although Mom and Aunt Yolanda did a good job of trying to let me know that it wasn't my fault that she got sick, I still felt bad anyway.

"Don't be proud of me, Ma."

"Yasmin, why do you say that?"

"Because all of the thoughts in my heart aren't pure."

"Honey, I don't know what you mean. I know you've been through a lot, but don't be so overdramatic about everything."

"I'm not making any of this up. Maybe God just doesn't love me."

"Why would you even say that, Yasmin?"

"Because, Ma, it's one thing after another. If I see another ambulance or hospital, I'm going to scream."

"Things happen in life but God uses them to bring us closer to Him. This isn't a punishment. It doesn't mean you did something wrong. What's been happening doesn't mean He loves you any less." Mom was trying to straighten me out. She went and got a Bible and turned to the book of Job.

"Ma, I'm sorry but I really don't feel like reading the Bible."

"Maybe that's my fault. I haven't gotten into the Word with you guys enough. I can't blame you for the way you're feeling. I been there and done that too, but now I'm trying to learn the right way and I think I've got it. The only way a mother can survive is to get a hold of what God's doing. And in the book of Job, there was a man who had a lot and then lost a lot. But in all he went through Yasmin there is a great lesson."

"I don't understand, Ma," I said as she flipped to the book of Job.

"Sometimes it's not God testing us, it's Satan," she said. "He is trying to steal from us and kill us; he wants to destroy us. We got to stand on God's Word and let Satan know that he can't have us."

"So, what happened with Job?" I asked.

"Come here. I want you to read Job 1 and 2."

I huffed and I puffed because the absolute last thing I wanted to do was read the Bible. I mean, she wanted me to know the story. Why couldn't she just tell me? But then as I started reading, I started comprehending what it said in the Word, and this story was so interesting.

God told the Devil that he wouldn't be able to kill Job or make him deny the name of the Lord. Sure enough, the Devil tried to make Job disown God by taking everything away from him. Even Job's wife said he should not believe in God anymore, and that was sort of how I felt. God had hurt me so many times or allowed Satan to hurt me so many times, what did I need Him for? But, Job stood strong and believed God even when things were really bad for him. And he said, "Blessed be the name of the Lord." He was saying that God gave him stuff and God takes stuff away. Even in all of that and through all that, he was still going to praise His name.

That did something to my soul. It did something to my spirit. Yes, my brother Jeff was gone. But God had given us his baby girl, Angel. Yes, my earthly father was in jail. But God allowed him to stay in touch with me, to let me know that I am loved. God had given my mom enough help to make sure we were taken care of. One thing happened after another but through it all, God showed up. It was good to be reminded that He loved me.

I went to my mom, laid my head on her chest, and said, "Thank you for showing me the way."

"Girl, I'm just pointing you to the truth. This world is tough, but it ain't no other way to make it. With God on your side, you can stay pure. I don't want you to turn to drugs and alcohol. I want you to have high self-esteem. But me as your mom wanting these things for you can't keep you pure forever. Yes, I can pray it up; and yes, God can answer my prayers. But, deep inside you, Yasmin Peace, you have got to want to stay pure. You have to want to please God and do the right thing because you know beyond a shadow of a doubt that He's looking out for you."

My mom was right. The Devil might try to test me, but I had to know that Jesus, God the Father, and the Holy Spirit were the only way for me. Pleasing the Lord gave me joy inside my heart.

"I want to help Alyssa find this kind of happiness," I said.

"But you got to be strong in your own faith, you got to believe first. You are going to be tested and you are going to be tried through all of that, but you can't help anybody else if you're going to sink back into your own flesh so easily."

"What do you mean, Ma?"

"Well, I talked to Aunt Yolanda and she said you guys were just throwing cans at each other, saying this and saying that."

"She just got on my nerves, Ma, blaming me."

"Yeah, but it also seems like you blamed yourself. You might be the only Christ some people will ever see."

"I don't understand what you mean."

"I mean, you talk about wanting to win your cousin to Christ. Let her know how awesome God is so she won't want to stay on the crazy path that she's on. You'll only alienate her by falling subject to the verbal attacks that she throws at you. Be the bigger person and make God not only proud by your words but by your actions too."

Mom kissed my forehead and her action showed that she was proud of me. And that felt good.

⊰⊱

Mom looked so sad. We were about to head back to Jacksonville, but before we did we stopped by to see Big Mama in the nursing home.

Big Mama didn't even know us, and though my mother was strong, I knew it tore her apart. I didn't know much about Alzheimer's but getting older and forgetting all or a lot of things that had gone on in your life couldn't be easy. Though my grandmother was still here, a part of her was wasting away. For a lady who had been so vibrant and wise for so many years, it just didn't seem right.

"Ma, Big Mama's going to be okay," I said when we got back in the car, not really believing those words myself.

"It's just a lot right now, baby. Before we go, we need to stop by the jail so we can see your dad. I really don't have time to do this, but he asked me to come by. Plus, I know you want to see him."

All of a sudden I felt really nervous. I hadn't even told Mom that I had already seen my dad. She didn't know that I had talked to him and all that good stuff. And I wasn't trying to hide it from her or anything like that. But I could tell she wasn't too happy about taking the time out to visit with Dad anyway.

"What's wrong with you? You don't wanna see your dad? It's all right. We're only going to be there for a minute. I know you don't like jails."

I looked out the passenger window. I didn't want her to see my face. Mom always knew when I was holding something back from her.

"Yasmin, talk to me."

"Okay, okay, I'll just tell you."

"Tell me what?"

"I just saw daddy on my birthday."

"You can't go to the jail. You're a minor."

"Well, I went with Alyssa and the man that ran the illegal electronics operation. It was all a setup. I didn't know that I couldn't go alone. I didn't realize you had to be there with me. You never said I couldn't go and see him. And Alyssa convinced me it was a great present for me to see him."

"Well, we talked a couple of times. You never mentioned that you saw him. I didn't think we had secrets like that, Yasmin."

"I'm sorry, Mom. I should have told you," I said knowing she was right.

"So you ended up going with Alyssa. How did y'all even get to the jail? This man picked you up too?"

"No, ma'am. We rode the bus."

"Well, he never told me either. I should have known. Did he even ask who brought you?"

Wishing I didn't have to reveal the truth, I hesitantly said, "No ma'am."

The rest of the way to the jail my mom was silent. I knew her well enough to know she wasn't happy. When we got into the closed-off quarters, my dad came in. Mom had attitude written all over her face.

"Vette, I really wanted to see you. I really need your help," Dad pleaded.

"Like all them years I needed your help and you couldn't help me because you were in here. Now you need something from me?"

"What's up with all the attitude?" Dad asked.

"Hey, Daddy," I said, interrupting them and giving him a big hug.

"Why didn't you tell me that she came to see you?" Mom asked, putting her hand on her hip.

"I thought you knew. I was just excited," Dad replied.

"You never even asked her any specific questions. How do you think she got here? How did you think she was able to see you? She's a minor."

"I thought Yolanda brought her," Dad answered, confirming what I knew he thought.

"Is that what you told him, Yasmin?" Mom questioned me.

"No, I didn't say anything."

"Then, wait a minute. What am I missing?" Dad asked.

"Your daughter came in here with some man that's been stealing and using underaged kids to help him."

Dad was getting furious. "Stealing? What! We talked about Yasmin making the right choices, but I didn't know she was even close to getting involved in something like that. I'm so sorry. You know I wouldn't have condoned anything like that! Who is he and has he been stopped? Yasmin, did you steal for him?"

"No, Daddy."

"Well, is he in jail or what? What's goin' on, Vette?"

"Listen, I'm just finding out details myself. If you wasn't in this place, maybe this wouldn't have happened. What is it that you want anyway, Jeffery? I got to get back on the road. I got to go and see about them boys."

My father shook his head and said, "You're right. If I wasn't in here, a lot would be different. That's why I wanted to tell you that my parole hearing is coming up in a couple months, and I really need you guys to be here as character witnesses. The judge knows that I got family who loves and needs me and that I need to get back to, so maybe he'll let me out."

"You still have two more years on your sentence," Mom said to him.

"Ma, what are you saying, you want him to stay in jail?" I asked, unable to keep quiet.

"Stay out of this, Yasmin! I'm talking to your father."

"You don't got to yell at the girl." Dad defended me.

"You not around to tell me what I need to do. Okay?" Mom shot back.

"Look, babe," Dad said. He walked over to my mom and placed his hands around her waist.

Before he could say any more, Mom stepped away and started in on him, "Get back. Don't be over here slick talking me with your cool moves, trying to get me to do what you want. We're not married anymore. The judge can look at the papers and see that. You're on your own. If you get out of here, great, but we can't count on that. And certainly you can't count on us to help you. I mean, Yancy can't even stand your guts. What's he gonna say? Your daughter's hanging out with somebody who'll be sharing a jail cell with you.

What kind of witness can she be? . . . sneaking in here to see her dad."

Dad continued his plea. "Vette, I just need your help. I just want a second chance at life. I know I messed up. I know I hadn't done everything right but I paid a lot of time for that. I want to get out so that I can make a difference in my kids' lives. You're right, I haven't been there. It's been my own fault but does that mean I don't deserve a second chance? I know it's not going to be easy. If I do get out, I got to make amends with my kids. I got to try and find a job, and I want you to trust me again."

"You need to hold your breath on that last one, babe," she said to him.

It was clear to me that Dad wanted to hang out with Mom again, but she had moved on. I knew she had feelings for Myrek's dad. I didn't know how deep all of that went, but this was clearly a lot of drama.

"Jeffery, I gotta go." she said to him and then saw how disappointed he and I both looked. "All right, I'll think about it."

Dad made one last appeal. "Thanks, Vette; that's all I can ask. The court's supposed to write you and let you know when the hearing is going to be. I need you there, Vette. I need the kids there. They might hate my guts, but you know I'm a man. I've changed a lot since I've been in here, and I love my babies. Shoot, I love you. You can blame me for a lot of things. All I'm asking is for you to come testify on my behalf and be a defender of truth."

Chapter 8

Answer Me, Please

I couldn't tell you how excited I was to be back at home. But it was a different home. It was a clean home with freshly painted walls and new furniture. So much had been donated by the community and the apartment manager. And not only did we have space, but we had three bedrooms. I had my own room! It felt so good, more than I could have imagined.

My mom only had time to drop me off and then head to work. However, it didn't take me long to notice that there was much tension between my brothers. Yancy was occupying my space to avoid bunking with York. He gave me a quick hug and said, "I sure don't want to share a room. The last person I want to stay with is York."

"Like my feelings gon' be hurt!" York yelled out from the other bedroom.

"Okay, so can I see the two of you guys?" I asked.

"Wait, I'm on the Xbox," York called out.

I peeked into his room and couldn't believe he had a TV and a game system hooked up in there. "I know, right? This is tight. I got a whole bunch of gifts from people in the community, telling me thanks. All legit, sis, so don't even look over here cross-eyed."

"No, seriously, that's great. But I want to talk to you guys," I said.

Yancy was already in a chair and York plopped down on the couch. His arm wasn't bandaged up anymore and though he had a skin graft, I could tell he was always going to have a slight scar. But it was great to see him better.

"Will somebody answer me and tell me what the heck is going on with you two? The tension is so thick a chainsaw couldn't cut it."

"Oh, that's what you wanted to talk to us about? Ask him," Yancy said, throwing a pillow from the chair to the floor.

"You're such a whiny baby. Don't nobody got time for all that," York said.

"Wait, wait, wait." I pulled Yancy back into the room before he stepped into the kitchen. "Guys, we're family. We need to be there for each other. Talk to me."

"Don't call him my brother," Yancy said. "He's a traitor. I'm glad you're back, Yasmin, for real. And though we got a fly place, I'm not gonna act like I'm thrilled to be here. So don't even try to make me."

I tried to reach out and hug him, but he jerked away and went out the front door. I sat down in the chair that he left behind.

Before I could say anything to York, Yancy opened the door again and came back inside. Obviously, he had thought about it and wanted to express himself.

"You know what? Let me set the record straight because I'm sick and tired of everybody thinking York is such a great guy, such a great hero, such a stud. He is selfish and only out for himself. Whatever he wants, he thinks he's entitled to."

York was sitting on the couch and just started laughing—almost like he was egging Yancy on.

"What is this about, y'all?" I asked in frustration.

"He took my girl, that's what." Yancy went back out the door and slammed it hard this time.

"What is he talking about?" I asked.

"Exactly. I mean, he's the one that broke it off with Veida."

"No. No, York. Pleeeeease tell me you are not talking to her?"

York tried to explain himself. "I ain't intended to. I mean, I know he tried to act like he don't care about her. Then as soon as anybody else talks to her, he gets his feelings hurt and stuff."

"But, that's your brother's ex-girlfriend," I said, trying to reason with him. "Aren't there certain rules Jeff told you guys about a long time ago and you said you'd always comply with them? Y'all got into it a long time ago about her. Jeff would be disappointed if he were here."

"Yeah, but if you recall, I was the first one who saw her. She and I made contact."

I corrected him. "No, she and Yancy met in school and they connected first. Besides, Veida promised me that she wouldn't come between you guys anymore. How did this happen?"

"Like I said, I ain't go asking for it. But, I mean, you know, if there's a connection, what you gon' do? When we were at her party and people were looking for you, some guys from her old school were picking on her or whatever. I just stepped in and got the guys straight. I caught her crying a few minutes later and she wound up in my arms. I mean, what can I say? One thing led to another and we been talking every day since," York explained.

"Talking how? Since when do we have a phone?"

"Yeah, girl we finally got a new line put in, plus I got my own cell. You know, I got the hookup from Bone." York went on to tell me more. "I wasn't trying to hurt Yancy's feelings. I wasn't even gonna mention it to him. I mean, because me and Veida were just friends. We were just talking. And I guess she was having some issues at home and I just happened to be here. I mean, we've been connecting."

York was pretty matter of fact about the whole thing. "Then he came home one day and saw her number on the caller ID, thought he had missed her call, and called her back. When she answered, she hollered out my name, thinking it was me. He jumped in my face and I punched him in his."

"What?! When did that happen?" I asked.

"A couple of days ago."

"York, you got to fix this. He's your brother."

"The way I see it, I think he stole the girl from me in the beginning. What's mine is mine. Plus, he said he didn't even want her. I ain't gon' give this up right now. We might have something and we might not. I'm not that deep into it, but I'm not gon' walk on eggshells to try and protect his feelings either. You wanted an answer. That's the truth. Deal with it, sis, or you can be ticked at me as well. I don't care."

Then York got up and went back into his room to play some stupid game. I didn't know if I was happy to be at home or not, but I was back and I had to find a way to fix this.

Later that night, Mom said there was a big youth rally at church and Kirk Franklin was going to perform. I was really excited to go and invited Asia to tag along. She and her mom were still having some type of issues. Though I might not have the answers to all of life's crazy questions, I sure do know the One who does.

The pastor got up to the podium and said, "Listen, young people. You guys are having it tough right now. Particularly in this part of Jacksonville where we live, crime is high. The high school graduation rate is down. We're killing each other. If you don't grab a hold to your future, if you don't try to make a change, and if you don't try to stand up for what God has for you, then you're not gonna be able to make it. You'll end up being another statistic and that's not good enough. That is not why we're here."

I looked over at Asia and she looked like a sponge, wanting to soak up every word that the pastor had to say. She needed to be encouraged; I needed to be lifted up. We both needed to focus on something higher so our problems wouldn't seem so bad.

"Teens, you may be out there and you may be going through a ton of problems. You may think that God has forgotten you. You may just want answers on how to fix all your trouble. I wish that I could tell you that life is going to be easy and that God is gonna have you go through life with no trials. But know that He wants to use whatever you're going through to bring you closer to Him. You can go though anything because you've got God in your heart helping you get through it.

"The Word says that 'greater is he that is in you, than he that is in the world.' The greater One is in you. And if you're here today and you don't have a personal relationship with God, if He isn't your Savior, if you're at your wit's end and you want Jesus to come into your heart so that the Holy Spirit can fight your battles for you, then I encourage you to come to the altar right now. Try it God's way. Know that only He can supply all your needs. He can do it."

Right away, Asia stood to her feet with watery eyes. I didn't have to move. I was amazed to see the urgency she had in going around me on her own. She went to the altar and laid it all there.

When we came out of church, the Lord wasted no time in moving. Her mother was there, waiting for her with her arms outstretched. Asia fell into them. No words were said, but I knew deep in my heart that the Lord had revealed to Asia's mom what a sneak her stepfather was. I didn't know how it was gonna all work out, but I knew Asia had it going on. She had her heavenly Father and her earthly mom. She was set.

⊰⊱

The next night all the teams in the apartment complex were on the basketball court having playoff games. I wanted to wish Myrek well, but every time I went over toward his way, he ended up talking to someone else, walking in the other direction, or something. I mean, he had seemingly no desire to come my way so that we could talk.

Seeing him, though, I got goose bumps. I knew that I wanted him to be more than my friend, but I had to play this the right way. I had to please God and that was way more important than giving Myrek whatever he might think he wanted. Even though by looking at his actions, it looked like he wanted nothing from me.

Asia came over and said, "Hey, girl," with a bright smile. She looked completely opposite of the way she did the day before at church. "You are a real good friend. Going to church was just what I needed. My mom, stepdad, and I have some things to work through; they care about how I feel and I know God's going to help us work it all out."

"That's great," I said.

"Yasmin, it's so nice how you can have your own problems but still care about your friends. I hope I can grow to be like that."

I wondered what she meant. I mean, it seemed like I always had some kind of drama going on, but Asia seemed to be talking about something specific.

"What do you mean, Asia?" I asked.

"You know, how Myrek has that new girlfriend now."

"A girlfriend? I didn't know that. I knew Myrek wasn't paying me no attention but—"

Asia cut me off. "Well, I thought you knew."

I started coughing. I needed to hear more details. When did this happen? What was going on? How could it be? He liked me. Who was this person? All of these questions flooded my mind.

"Veida told me it's some girl that she used to go to school with," Asia offered.

"So, the girl is gonna be going to our school next year?" I asked, as we half watched the basketball game.

"Yeah, we're all going to the same high school. I met her at the party after you left. Supposedly, she's been hounding him. You hadn't called him or anything like that, so I think they're going out."

"Is she cute, ugly, what?" I wanted to know.

"Well . . . she's gorgeous. I mean, I'm not trying to hurt your feelings with this or anything." Asia was just being painfully honest.

Myrek went up for a layup, but he dunked the ball instead, and the crowd started cheering. He was becoming "the man." And because I had snoozed just a little, it looked like the ship had sailed without me. As he came to the sideline, he looked over at me. I guess he saw in my eyes that something wasn't right, like I'd just gotten news that broke my heart. He left the game and people started booing.

He walked straight over to me and said, "Let's talk." We went walking down the street, but stayed in view of everyone. I was conscious of what my mom had told me a few weeks back. She said that a young lady had to maintain her reputation. And since everyone saw us walk off, it was no need to start any rumors. I planned to stay in their sight and keep it that way.

Once we had a little peace away from the crowd, I said, "I thought it was gonna be you and me."

"I thought it was gonna be us too. You go out of town for weeks and don't call me. You kissed me when I found you in the woods, then you said it was a mistake. You confused me so much, Yasmin Peace. You don't want none of this," Myrek responded.

"Just because I'm confused, just because I wanna do it the right way doesn't mean that I don't want to be with you. It doesn't mean that I'll have a connection with you. But that doesn't mean I don't want to try and figure this out. I mean, couldn't you have given me the benefit of the doubt of trying to do that before you moved on?"

"Who says I moved on?" Myrek asked.

"Don't play me, Myrek. I just heard you got some new girlfriend, some girl that's come from the other school."

He looked away. "Oh, you heard that?"

"Are you denying it? Is it not the truth?"

"You know what? You and I don't have any ties to each other. You just wanted to be friends, so you got your wish. Don't worry about what I'm doing and don't act like you really wanna be with me when you don't really know what being with me really means. Everything can't be on your terms. I got feelings too. You just ignore them, Yasmin."

"Well, the way you want to handle them is just not gonna work for me. Do you have a girlfriend or not? Do we even have a chance? Can't we just figure out what's going on?" I asked.

He just walked away when folks started calling his name to come back to the court. I was so frustrated, I could've screamed. But the only thing that came out was, "Answer me, please!"

Chapter 9

Uglier than Ever

So, I guess this was it. Myrek turned away from me and walked back toward the crowd. He didn't care that I'd asked him a question, and he wasn't giving me an answer. For a moment that was all right, but then I thought long and hard. We'd been friends way too long. We did have feelings for each other. I wasn't imagining it. He pursued me. If nothing more, he owed it to me to tell me what the heck was going on.

Did he have a girlfriend or not? I wanted to know so I jogged in front of him, pushed him backwards away from the crowd and said, "Look, dude, be real. You're with somebody now? Tell me."

"Why you gotta be all up in my business and why you gon' try to front me in front of these people? Quit pushing on me, Yasmin."

Then he tried to walk around me, but I stepped in his path again. I kept my hands to myself. I could hear what he was saying and he was much bigger than me, not that I thought he'd hurt me or anything. But I didn't want to embarrass him. I just looked at him. As the streetlights glared on my face, he could see that I was sincere. I needed an answer. I needed to know something. Did he have a girlfriend or not?

"Yeah, okay. Is that what you wanna hear? You want me to hurt your feelings and say yeah? All right. There it is. I got somebody now."

Thankfully, he didn't walk toward the crowd. He completely turned around and walked back in the direction we'd come from. He wasn't talking to me, but he wasn't going toward everybody else. So I figured he knew that we needed to talk about this. He knew I just wasn't gonna leave it alone. He knew we had to discuss it.

"So, could you at least wait up?" I called out from behind him.

"Yasmin, I'm just going this way because I want to think, okay? I don't wanna talk to you about anything, and I certainly don't wanna argue."

I jogged to get beside him. "You know that I can't go with you down any further into this darkness, so could you please just stop so we can talk about everything? You got a girlfriend now. Who is she and why couldn't you wait on me?"

"Wait on you?" he said in the meanest tone I'd ever heard him sound. "I gave you plenty of chances to get with this. All you did was brush me off. You heard what I said, but you did whatever you wanted to do, and that was to completely stay away from me. So now that I'm interested in somebody else, all of a sudden you got issues."

"Do you really like her?" I asked.

Myrek laid it all on the line. "Her name is Raven and she doesn't nag me, and she's really, really cute. She's not sitting there talking about what God wants to do all the time. She let's me know she likes me, and she doesn't try to play no games. A lot of other boys are trying to get with her, but she wants me."

"She just wants you because she thinks you're gonna be some kind of basketball star."

"And, what? You tryin' to say I'm not?" he challenged me.

Everything that I said, he was taking it and making it real personal. But how could I blame him? All that he said hurt me to the core and it was personal to me too. If Myrek never played a game of basketball again, I would still have these "up in the air," some kind of big, deep feelings for him.

Even though I couldn't really put my thoughts around what all that was supposed to be for us, one thing I was sure of, it didn't have to do with his popularity. I knew who he was, what made him mad, and what his favorite foods are. He used to think that I was the prettiest girl he'd ever seen, and now he stands here telling me that someone else took my place in his heart. I tried as hard as I could to fight back the water that welled up in my eyes. I couldn't let him see me upset. I couldn't let him see me mad. I couldn't let him see me cry. But, I cried anyway.

Then he sounded off. "What? You think just because I see tears, I'm gonna break up with her? You might, Yasmin, but I ain't tryin' to wait all my life for nothing. You stay over there and wait on Jesus. I ain't tryin' to be frustrated like my dad, okay? I'm done with the Peace women."

Now he had really taken his remarks to a rude level. And it didn't take a rocket scientist to know he was alluding to the fact that his dad had not had sex with my mom. Though I was really thankful for that, I was somehow agitated that they'd even discussed it in the first place. And, if they hadn't discussed it, that his father would be so carefree to let out his feelings around his son.

I'm glad he was done with the Peace women. The Myrek that I knew, or thought I knew so well, had changed in a big way. And now I was done with his tail too. I wiped my eyes that were full of real and genuine tears, held my head up high, and walked back toward the crowd.

"Oh, what? You just gonna walk away like that?" he demanded.

I was determined not to say another word. He went on, "Just make sure you don't try nothing crazy when we get to school in a couple of months, because Raven Floyd is a gorgeous dark-skinned sister that you can't hold a candle to."

Yeah. I kept all my thoughts to myself and kept on walking. I prayed with each step, *Lord, this is hard to hear and hard to take in. I feel like my stomach is on a roller-coaster ride, dropping ten thousand feet and it won't end. I feel sick. It ain't a pretty situation, but I know You'll help me stay true to me and help me get through all this hurt.*

When I got back to the court, Asia came over to me and said, "Can I spend the night with you, Yas?"

"I doubt it, my mom ain't gon' let me have no company like that."

"I'm not really tryin' to stay the night with you. You see Jack, that fine man over there?"

"Yeah, that boy who's going to the twelfth grade?" I asked.

"Yeah, girl, he likes me."

"What? He just tryin' to be grown," I said to Asia.

"What, you sayin' I don't have it going on enough that a senior wouldn't want to be with me?"

"Okay, so now you gonna take it personally, Asia? Getting all up in my face and telling me that he's interested in you. Well, I don't think so."

"Well, look. That's fine. Think what you want. I know I can make it work with him," she said with a big attitude.

"How do you even know Jack?" I asked her.

"When I was living at my cousin's house, he would come over."

"Then, why don't you go over to your cousin's house?"

"Well, now that I done moved out, they want their space and all of that stuff," Asia explained.

"That's what you need to do. Have somebody over with some supervision."

"Yasmin, quit trying to tell me what to do. I just need you to be my friend now, all right? My mama likes you. Shoot, we went to church together."

"Yeah, and you gave your heart to God. Both of us need to focus on pleasing Him. We need to forget these boys."

"You're just jealous, Yasmin."

"Are you serious?" I said.

Asia shot back at me. "See, you always think you better than everybody else. Just because he ain't as handsome as Myrek, or cute like your brothers, you gonna sit there and say he ain't got nothing going on. Let me tell you, honey, he is gonna be a senior and he's got plenty going on."

"So, what?" I challenged her.

She took her hand and lifted it to hit me, but I took mine and stopped it in the process. In my mind, I thought, *You know what?*

*That's what I get for letting my guard down and thinking I could have
a good girlfriend, a guy, or anybody for that matter!*

What I really needed was to just stay closed off like I'd been
most of my life, not worry about what other people thought, and
not let anybody steal my joy.

"So, you not gonna help me?" Asia asked in a panicked voice.

"You just wanted to hit me! I know you not gonna ask me that
again. No, I'm not gonna help you, and I don't care if we're not
friends anymore. There! There you go." I had raised my voice in
anger.

"You just mad at me because Myrek left you."

I wasn't about to let her get away with that. "Myrek couldn't
leave me because we were never together. Get your facts straight,
Asia."

"Well, I know you mad because I got a boyfriend." She wouldn't
let up.

"Oh, so Jack's your boyfriend now? Whatever. Forget you."

"Cool. Forget you too," Asia said. She went back over to Jack
and hugged him. I walked home alone.

I was knocked out asleep when my mom came into my room
and asked if I knew where Asia was. I was half-asleep and said,
"Uh, uh. Ma, I'm tired. I'm sorry, no."

Then Asia's mother came into my room. "Yasmin, please wake
up, dear. Asia told me that she was staying with you. I tried to get
her to confirm it when I called her on her cell, but she gave me the
runaround. I heard a boy's voice in the background. Something just
told me to get up and come over here to see for myself. So, you mean
to tell me that she hadn't spent the night over here? You don't know
where she is or who the boy is that I heard through the phone?"

I didn't know what to say, I mean, I was tired but at that moment I was completely alert. I had two choices. I could tell the truth and let the chips fall wherever they may. That would really backup what I said to Asia when I told her that I didn't care and I wasn't gonna cover for her. Or, I could help her by doing whatever I could to stop her and salvage all of this craziness that she left for me to clean up.

Then, of course, I had to factor in that piece with my mom's hand on her hip, shaking her head and looking me dead in my eye like I better tell the truth and not cover for nobody. What in the world was a girl to do? This was a hot mess.

Lord, I prayed as I looked at two upset women, *I know I said that I was mad at Asia and I know we said a lot of hot stuff to each other, but I do care about her and I don't want her to get into trouble. Even though I told her she couldn't stay with me, she's using me as a cover-up anyway! So, I am mad. But I need You to help me be honest, but still not sell her down the river. She's already sinking. I'm just trying to help her not drown. That's not wrong, is it?*

Then I thought about it, *When I left her, I didn't know where she went.* So, when I told Asia's mother that I didn't know where she was, it wasn't a complete lie. But, I knew that I was walking a thin line. Though both Asia's mom and mine were angry, they couldn't force me to say more. I turned over and went back to sleep, praying that Asia knew what she was doing.

The next day about noon she called me, crying.

"Thank you. Thank you for telling my mom really nothing."

"Asia, what's—why are you crying?"

"When Jack dropped me off, after I went further than I should have gone, he told me that he didn't want to see me again. He said that he has a girlfriend and she's also a senior at our school. I feel so stupid and used. And now my mom hates me too because I lied to her. I feel used up with no love."

"I love you, girl," I said, knowing that wasn't going to be enough to mend her broken heart.

Later that night, Mom was getting dressed to go out. I'd really been thinking about Myrek's little snob comment about his dad wanting to go far and my mom didn't. I mean, Myrek knew they were adults and Mom wasn't married to his dad. I was proud of her for taking a stand and practicing what she preached to me. But he couldn't appreciate that; he had an issue with it.

I needed to let her know that I wasn't giving her any drama about going out with Mr. Mike. After all, I was her kid and she probably would put me in my place even if I tried. But there were some things about him that she needed to know. I was not gonna keep my mouth shut because if it was the other way around, I would want her to tell me. So I went to her door and knocked on it.

"Ma, can I come in please?"

"Yeah, baby, I'm just getting ready. But, I don't have much time to talk. What's going on?"

"I heard from Asia today."

"Oh, good. Is that girl all right? Her mom was so mad. Don't you ever go—"

"I know, Ma. I won't. I won't, trust me. She learned a hard lesson."

"What do you mean?"

I remembered the times in sixth and seventh grade when I was able to tell my mom stuff about girls and we would talk in depth about it. We talked about how naive girls can be sometimes, how they let boys walk all over them without really understanding that guys say one thing and then, as soon as they get what they want, they do something completely different.

So, I went there and said, "Ma, I really need to talk to you about you."

"What do you mean, honey?"

"Mr. Mike. I mean this date and stuff. I got some issues with it."

"Oh, honey, come on. I know you were down there talking with your dad this summer. And you've got this fancy thought of us getting back together. Even if he gets out, I'm still moving on with things."

"Yeah, that's part of it," I said as I held my head down. I hadn't forgotten that Dad still wanted to try and get back with Mom. But, that wasn't the reason I came to talk to her. Even though it was a really important reason and she should consider that there was a man out there who truly loves her.

And, if he did love her, then why was he having a problem because he wasn't getting everything he wanted? Why couldn't he wait on her? And would he try to rush my mom into marrying him without really loving her, just to get what he wanted?

Ugh, all this was really making me angry. I wanted Mom to be happy, but I wanted her to be happy going out with him and knowing the truth about him. I wanted her to know the whole story and all that was going on.

"Ma, Mr. Mike . . . I'm sure he wants to . . . you know, get with you . . . have sex."

"What did you say to me? Girl, you better watch your mouth."

"Okay, okay, I might be talking too casually, but there was a time when you told me I could tell you anything," I reminded her.

"Yeah, you can tell me anything but you still need to preseent your point respectfully," she scolded me.

"I mean, I'm just saying. Myrek told me that his dad wants to go further. You know what I mean. He's pretty mad with y'all just going out because he's spending his money on you, and y'all not taking it all the way."

"Did he say all of that?"

"Well, no. Not in those exact words, but he sort of hinted around it."

"Come on, Yasmin," she said impatiently.

"No, Ma, I'm serious. I'm not crazy. You always said I got good sense. I know what people are thinking and Mr. Mike is upset. I don't think you should go out with him anymore. I mean, I haven't even discussed this with York and Yancy, but they are gonna flip when they hear that he wants to really, really get with you."

"Listen, little girl," my mom said, pointing her lipstick all up in my face. "You don't need to be discussing my business with your brothers. All y'all need to stay out of my affairs. I know what I'm doing. I'm grown. If Mike has any issues with the way our rela-tionship is going, we'll discuss them and move on.

"And what he says behind closed doors about him being frus-trated with our involvement is his problem. He ain't saying it to my face and that's what you gotta understand, little lady. Yeah, he's gonna want things, yeah he might not always get his way, but so what. As long as I don't go along with it, and as long as we can work through our drama, then it's no big deal."

"Ma, I just don't want you to go out with him and there be a whole bunch of tension. Please."

"Let me handle this stuff, Yasmin."

"I know, Ma. I'm just saying. Please be careful."

"Listen, let me handle me. Let me take care of my life. I understand you being concerned, and there is nothing wrong with you being worried about your mama. But I know when I'm in too deep, and I know all that I can handle."

She put on a cute dress and grabbed her purse. Then the doorbell rang. When she went to answer it and opened the door, Mr. Mike stepped in and gave her a big hug and kiss. That's when I really knew that I was gonna have to do something to stop this before Mom went down a wrong road and that she wouldn't be able to get back on the right track. This was way past what I felt was acceptable. Things were uglier than ever.

Chapter 10

Harder
We Fell

*I*t was now August. I had no idea where July went, but I was getting excited that school was about to begin, and soon I would be off to high school. My modeling classes were about to start in a week. Actually, I had been pretty bored in the house. There hadn't been much to do and I wasn't babysitting little Angel. I was at my crib kind of enjoying my own room. But with Mom at work and my brothers into who knows what, a change of scene wouldn't be so bad. The phone rang and I grabbed it instantly.

"Hello? Hello?" I said hurriedly into the receiver.

"What's wrong? You sleep?" Asia asked.

"It's just getting late. I was dozing off. What's up?"

"What's up is that I was wondering if you're going down to Lee Road."

"Why would I be going down there where those gangbangers hang out?" I asked.

"Girl, it's gonna be a gang fight tonight. That's why," she announced.

"Oh, and I really want to be all up in the middle of that," I replied sarcastically.

"You should want to be. You notice your brothers ain't home, right?"

"They're just down the street. They'll be home soon," I said.

"Not until after the fight goes down tonight."

"How do you know that? What are you talking about?"

"It's Bone's crew against Romeo's crew . . . they're fighting over territory. Supposedly, somebody is selling on somebody else's corner," Asia informed me.

"I ain't heard nothin' about that. And what does that have to do with York and Yancy?" I said to Asia, trying to dismiss the fact that she always talked junk. She always tried to stir up stuff, and she ain't even need to go there 'cause there wasn't nothing even going on. With all the drama she'd had in her life recently, she needed to just chill.

"My brother ain't hanging with Bone no more," I told her.

"Girl, yes he is!"

"He ain't slinging no rock," I said with assurance.

"Nah, but they're selling guns. My cousin told me. 'Cause, you know, her husband is one of their suppliers."

"No, I didn't know that," I admitted.

"Yeah. That's another reason why my mama didn't want me living over there any more. It's just too dangerous," Asia added.

I didn't want to admit it to her, but I immediately thought back to the time when we were at the school dance. I remembered seeing York with steel in his waistband. He was sort of showing it off.

"Come on! You need to go with me."

"Well, I just don't understand. You're talking about York,

though I don't believe you. But, what does that have to do with Yancy?"

"Well, word on the street is that he's kicking it with Romeo." She was just loaded with information.

"What?" I said in shock.

"Yeah, girl. Romeo was looking for somebody that could help him with his money and stuff, and he couldn't trust some of his own people. Everybody was talking about how smart your brother is. So, they been rollin' together for a couple of weeks now. Then somebody stepped on somebody's toes, and now they 'bout to throw down."

Asia liked to be in the middle of all the drama, but she wasn't someone that would make up something for no reason. I had to take what she was saying seriously. There was no way I could let Yancy and York be fighting each other in opposite gangs! Fists, knives, guns—those older dudes were too hard for my brothers to be around. Then all of a sudden, the door opened and it was York. I told Asia I had to go.

"Call me back! Call me back, girl!" she exclaimed.

I just went up and stood in his face and rolled my eyes as hard as I could. I had my hand on my hip like he owed me an explanation and needed to give me one right away.

"Yasmin, what you standing in front of me like that for? Like you're my mama. I gotta get something, and I gotta go."

"You can't go out there to a fight! Please!"

"Wha—" York started.

"Don't try to deny it. I know everything. You told Ma you wasn't hanging with Bone anymore and now you down with him—selling guns! York, you gon' be in jail!"

"They'll protect me. If anything goes down, they say they gon' take the rap. Romeo and them done stepped the wrong way and stole some of our stuff. We gotta claim it back," he said, trying to reassure me.

"I heard this was about some corner or some territory issue," I said, wanting to stall him.

"You need to just make sure you stay here tonight, Yasmin!"

"No, uh uh," I said, putting on my shoes. "You go out that door, and I'll do it too. And not that you care because you and Yancy haven't been speaking to each other, but you know he's hanging with Romeo."

"Nah, no way," he said in disbelief. "He be at the library and stuff."

"He's been counting Romeo's money." When I said that, York had a confused look on his face.

"I know you care, York. Even though y'all been going at it, and you're still talking to Veida."

"I ain't thinking about that girl!"

"Yeah, whatever! Y'all got tension. We done already been through enough than to see y'all get killed, cut, stabbed, beat up, or shot tonight. How is Ma supposed to survive that? I mean, you already survived a fire. You ain't no cat! You ain't got nine lives, York."

As soon as I said that, Mom walked in the door with Yancy. I hugged him as tightly as I could.

"What's wrong with you?" she said to Yancy as he fidgeted.

"Man, Ma, I told you I'd be back!" Yancy tried to convince her so that he could get away.

"Nah, you don't need to be out hanging with those suspects. I told your butt to get in the car, and that's what I meant. I'm glad I came home. I'm over here thinking y'all are okay and you out there in the streets. At least your brother and sister are here." Mom was right on time.

"I'm sure York just got here," Yancy said.

The two of them started looking at each other. I knew York wanted to ask Yancy questions about Romeo, but he couldn't in front of our mom. I loved the two of them so much, and I knew that they had issues with each other. They thought they were grown men, but they weren't.

So, I told Mom everything, and she put the house on lockdown. They were mad at me, but I didn't care that we fell out. At least they'd still be alive.

＜◎＞

Time was moving, and my brothers stayed on lockdown for four days. They were so irritable; they weren't getting along with each other at all. They were mad at my mother and me. I didn't know what they were saying behind their closed doors, but I knew it wasn't pretty. Most of it was because of Veida.

Uncle John and Aunt Lucinda brought little Angel over to spend some time with us. Mom was so glad because she had a few days off to take care of her granddaughter.

I was really happy to get out of my house a few days later. Being able to go to modeling class was something I so looked forward to. It was the start of a new session, and we were going to practice walking on the runway. Since I was pretty tall, I wasn't used to wearing heels. But I knew that I had to take them with me and wear them while I was there.

"Hey," Veida said, strolling over to where I was standing.

I just huffed. I was trying to give her a sign to let her know that I didn't want to talk to her or be around her. She needed to get out of my face. But she wouldn't move. She was so close I could actually smell her tart breath. If I'd had some breath mints, I would've shared them with her! Instead I walked away.

"You my girl! You just gon' not wanna be around me, not gon' care about me, forget all we had?" she asked me.

"Forget all we had?" I retorted. "You in it for only what you can get, Veida. You stay on that side of the class," I said, shooing her away. "I'll be over here."

"I mean, but, York has even pulled back some," she offered.

I didn't want to say anything to her, but that was a great thing for York to do. If it came down to choosing his brother over some girl, he needed to make the right choice and choose Yancy.

"You just like being at the center of attention, don't you?" I said when she wouldn't leave me alone.

"No! I told you, it just sorta happened. But now it looks like it's over. I mean, do I have to lose you too?"

"My family comes first, Veida. You know we've had it rough," I reminded her.

"But I've got it rough too!" she exclaimed.

"Yeah, but you give one excuse after another. You never take responsibility for anything. It's just like a repeated pattern with you, and somehow my family keeps getting pulled into it! If you're not jerking Yancy around, then you're trying to upset him with York."

"I wasn't being phony with what I was feeling, Yasmin."

"Okay, so you were real. What? And that's supposed to justify it? They are brothers and supposedly your good friend's brothers at that. You know how to do damage to our relationship, just like the first time we became friends. But there you go, only caring about how you feel! And you step right into it again." I was really fed up with her and let her have it.

"Your brothers are big boys, you know."

"Yeah, big boys who have a lot of frustration pent up inside of them. Their father ain't here. Their older brother is dead. Their mama's dating somebody who is tryin' to—just forget it," I said, trailing off.

She grabbed my arm. "No, no! Tell me. Who is tryin' to do what?"

"Forget it. We're not friends like that, all right? I'm glad York left you alone. I hope it's for good."

"So you just think I only care about me? Huh?" She asked me with eyes all watery. I didn't know where all the emotion was coming from, and I wasn't tryin' to be all up on a pedestal like I was judging her either. I knew one thing for sure. I wanted my actions to speak louder than my words so I just turned away. I went and sat down to listen to the instructor tell us how to walk and stride.

Ms. Hall said, "So, young ladies, modeling is all about confidence. Having confidence is important in making sure you make the garment look its best. No matter what anybody else thinks about you, you have to know that you're the bomb. Now, I don't mean overconfidence. I'm talking about positive energy—a joy that is irreplaceable. That means, if trouble comes your way, you don't lie down; you don't let it get you down. Your world doesn't shatter. You suck it up, move on, and adjust. You work it out! Let me see somebody in the room that can work it out with me. Put on a little music. Let's work it out. Yeah, confidence, ladies."

For some reason at that moment, I didn't have confidence. I just sat in my seat not wanting to get up, but then she called me out.

"You, young lady, come on! Let's go." And, when I got up on the runway and took three steps, I fell hard onto my butt. All the other seven girls laughed. I was so embarrassed that I got up and dashed to the bathroom. I was surprised to see Veida show up after all I had taken her through. But she had run after me.

"They just don't know," she said. "Once you get it together, you gon' be putting us all to shame."

"Why are you in here?" I prodded.

"I know you don't want me to be in here. I just wanted to tell you it was okay. Sometimes we don't get it right the first or second time, like in my case. That doesn't mean we aren't supposed to keep trying. We can't stay down. We gotta bounce back. I just wanted to come and say that." She turned around and walked away. I leaned my head on the bathroom stall and prayed.

Lord, I guess I'm just an idiot. Thanks for quickly showing me that I'm not perfect either. I can't believe Veida said what she did. We gotta keep tryin' to get it right. I focus so much on other people's issues, but help me find that joy within myself, to be a better me.

Lately, Mom had Uncle John spending a lot of time with my brothers. She told him that they were backsliding into trouble, and he stepped up to the plate. Since he'd been around, they'd been better. If they weren't on the basketball court or working out at the gym, they were cutting lawns in Uncle John's neighborhood. They actually hung out with each other and spent the night over there. So it was just me and Mom together the last week before school was to begin.

The doorbell rang, and my mom asked me to get it. It was Miss Sandra. She looked a hot mess like she had been sleeping in the streets or something. She was acting all jittery and couldn't seem to keep still.

"Come on in," I said hesitantly and called, "Ma!"

"Who is it, girl?" my mom yelled back.

"It's Miss Sandra."

"Let her in," my mom called from her room. "I'll be right there."

Miss Sandra paced back and forth in our apartment as if something was terribly wrong with her. I didn't want to think she was on drugs but I'd seen some folks around the way who were and knew exactly how they acted. I'd also seen enough movies and thought that a drug addiction was probably her case.

Miss Sandra started rambling. "They done took my babies, split them up, and won't give them to me."

"Ma!" I yelled out. I cared so much about those little ones that any news I heard about them really got me going.

"Ma!" I yelled again, feeling a little uncomfortable.

Miss Sandra just kept ranting and talking loudly.

"Girl, I'm right here, Yasmin. Goodness, gracious. What's the problem?"

When Mom saw her, she said, "Sandra, what is going on? You need to settle down! Yasmin, get her something cool to drink."

I went to the kitchen and opened the fridge. I moved the orange juice out of the way, grabbed the pitcher of lemonade, reached over for a glass on the counter, and came back to Miss Sandra.

"Here you go," I said, handing her the glass.

"All right. Thank you, thank you," she said still huffing and puffing.

"They said they gon' keep my babies! They gon' split them apart. They . . . they said I ain't fit—I ain't a good mama and I can't get them back. If they split up . . . I don't know what I'm gonna do, and—"

"It's okay, it's okay," my mom tried to console her.

"Yvette, you gotta take my babies! At least, if you got them I can come see about them. Or, if you got them, when I get myself together, I can . . . I can—"

"Calm down, Sandra," my mom said.

"No! No! You don't understand. I'm trying to get myself together and, when I do, then I can come and get them. And it don't matter what the system say! You'll help me like that, right? Right? You'll help me?"

"Come on now, Sandra, you gotta calm down," Mom said again.

Sandra took the glass and threw it across the room, shattering it into pieces and causing lemonade to splatter everywhere. Mom wasn't even upset but I was because I knew that I would have to clean it up.

Then I looked back at the lady who thought she was losing everything. I was so selfish. I didn't even want to clean up her mess, which would take me five minutes. With the mess she was in, she would clearly not be able to clean it up anytime soon—maybe ever.

"I'm sorry, but you can . . . you gotta go by there. You gotta call them, you gotta get my babies."

"Listen. I'm not going to get your babies so you can come here and take them. That wouldn't make it right. I don't have enough room here for those kids anyway. Besides, I'm barely here for my own children, and they got a ton of issues. I'd like to say I'm the world's greatest mama, but I'm not!"

"What am I gon' do? What am I gon' do? They can't take my babies! They can't pull them apart! Little Dante needs his sister. They need me!" she said in exasperation.

After a few tries, Mom finally got Miss Sandra to calm down. She told her to take a shower and gave her some clean clothes to put on. Then we went and visited a social worker who confirmed what Miss Sandra was saying. Unless they could find a home adequate enough that could take both kids, they were going to have to separate them. It was because the temporary foster care home that the kids were in didn't want them permanently.

Later on, we went over to Uncle John and Aunt Lucinda's house. As I held little Angel and rocked her, I heard Mom trying to convince them to take in two more kids. Of course, Aunt Lucinda was all for it. She had wanted a family for so long. This was an answer to prayer for her, but Uncle John wasn't having it.

"Then we'll have three kids. I'm already raising your kids with you, Yvette. This is enough right now," he said.

"I know," Mom explained. "And I wouldn't be asking you if I had another option. I'm trying to deal with my mother having Alzheimer's plus all my kids' drama. These are some good kids, and who knows where they'll end up if you don't help them. Just imagine if that little girl gets into the wrong hands or house. Or imagine if that little boy gets into a family where somebody terrorizes him. Come on, John, you got a heart! I ain't saying you gotta keep them forever, but they just need another good foster home for a while. Can't you get to know them?"

Mom succeeded in pleading her case. The next day the meeting was arranged. The kids were just coming over to Uncle John's to play. Uncle John sort of already knew Miss Sandra's kids, Randi and Dante, from the time he stayed at our house while Mom was out of town getting some job training.

We were able to be there, and it was so exciting when Randi ran up to me and gave me the biggest hug. Boy, had I missed that little girl. And the way that she adored little Angel was really special. Dante even slipped up and called Uncle John "daddy."

We barbecued on the grill and everyone was enjoying the day. York and Yancy were playing ball with each other and getting along. We all watched as my aunt and uncle bonded with the kids. Then suddenly, the social worker arrived to come and get them. Aunt Lucinda started to tear up.

"You think this might work?" the social worker asked them.

"Yes, let them stay," Aunt Lucinda said as she looked at her husband. He just nodded his consent.

"Very good. We'll go through all the process with you guys, and fill out the emergency home paperwork so they can stay here," the social worker replied.

Uncle John spoke up. "It's only been one day, and we can't let these precious babies go, as hard as I tried not to be all into them," Uncle John admitted.

I couldn't help but notice, if you looked at little Dante holding on to his leg, it was obvious that God was doing something big.

Uncle John even said, "It's something bigger than me. It's something we just gotta go with. I care for these kids like I never thought that I could. It has to be the Lord. The more I wanted to stay away from them—and the more my wife and I wanted this not to work—the harder we fell."

Chapter 11

Number One
Fan

I ain't no punk, Reverend Crane," my brother York said in Sunday school to our youth pastor. We were having a big discussion on how to act and how to represent God in high school.

"Naw. Come on, York," the cool, young Reverend Crane said. "I'm not asking you to be a wimp, but I am saying that you don't need to start nothing either. You don't need to judge people. You don't need to go to school with a chip on your shoulder. But you do need to act like God is in your heart."

Yancy was over in the corner being quiet like he didn't want to be there. Mom said that if there was ever a time when we shouldn't miss church, it was before we headed back to a new school year. It's not that I was hesitant. It's just that I didn't know the discussion would be so lively, so on point, so exactly what I needed. I really hated that I hadn't gone to church more throughout the summer. Reverend Crane always related to us on our level.

"Guys, God's Word is a road map, people. He can guide your

way. He wants to reign and rule in your life. He wants to fight your battles. He can change the heart of kings. He can change the heart of anybody," the reverend explained.

"I'm just keeping it real. I mean, I know me, my brother, and sister haven't been in your class in a while," York replied. "And, I'm down with God for real. I'm just saying, if somebody wants to try me, I can't let them think that because I am down with G-O-D that they can be all over me. You know what I'm saying?" York kept defending his position.

"Yeah, brother, I hear you," Reverend Crane said. "And you got a legitimate point, but it's still not a case you'd win. In God's Word, He says, 'Come unto me, all ye that labor and are heavy laden, and I will give you rest. Take my yoke upon you, and learn of me; . . . for my yoke is easy, and my burden is light.' That means, if you have any issues, drama, or problems that you think you can't solve, Jesus wants you to give it to Him and He will work it out for you. He's not saying He's going to leave you out there. If you read in the book of Matthew, verses 28–30 of chapter 11, Jesus is saying that He's got your back, your front, your sides—all that."

This cute, plump little girl named Tasha, who was eyeing my brother, raised her hand.

"Yes, Tasha, go ahead," Reverend Crane acknowledged.

"York has a good point because if you're in the middle of something and someone steps to you at school and they swing, then there's a big ol' crowd. It's like . . . what are you supposed to do? Wait, stop, and get on your knees and pray for God to work it out?"

Everybody started laughing.

"Y'all can be silly with it, if you want to," Reverend Crane said. "Ha ha, hee hee, . . . but you best believe that somewhere in the middle of that drama you can still take the high road."

"Yeah, and then people are going to laugh at you and think you're weak. You're going to get even more people coming at you," Tasha added.

"I just don't believe that, guys. God knows how to defend you and get His message across to anyone who tries to oppose you. And, for some reason, we are stuck on this thing about people wanting to fight," Reverend Crane added.

"What about going to school and making sure nobody is talking about anybody. You know, squashing it when your buddies are around you putting somebody else down. They want you to sign off on what they're saying like, 'Yeah, didn't she wear those same clothes yesterday?' And, most people's response will be what?" he asked.

Tasha spoke up, "Yep, she wore that same outfit yesterday."

Everybody laughed again.

Reverend Crane didn't back down. "Exactly," he said. "But what about not judging people because of their clothes? Honestly, for everything that you can say about somebody else, someone could find fault in you too. The Word says we've got to be our brother's keeper. Treat people like you like to be treated, do unto others as you'd have them do unto you, and all of that."

Then, he really gave me something to think about when he said, "And sometimes I believe that we don't think with our heart. While we are in school, we just allow ourselves to be popular at someone else's expense. I know all fifteen of you guys in this room, whether you've been to one Sunday school class or you've been to all of them that I've had this summer, you know better. Now, you got to get out there and do better." No doubt about it, Reverend Crane was making a lot of sense.

Yancy finally looked up and said, "What if you got issues with someone in your own family?"

The look that he shot at York was frightening. Chills went up my spine. My brothers had worked out a lot of stuff, but I knew there was still tension between them. And, in the house of the Lord, Yancy laid out all his cards. He was angry.

"It's tricky when you talk about family," Reverend Crane said. York laughed a little to try and avoid being embarrassed that his brother had issues with him. But, he couldn't avoid it; Yancy's point was directed right at him.

"All right, everybody, let's be respectful," Reverend Crane said, looking straight at York.

"As I was saying to Yancy, dealing with family can be very tricky. We are supposed to love them. We got to live with them and sometimes they do things that really hurt us. But, I guess that's why I'm trying to tell you guys you've got to check yourself. You can't control other people—but God can. You can only control how you respond to other people. If you keep looking at things from a godly perspective, then you'll start to allow His love to reign and rule in your lives. That will keep you from living under the Devil's influence of hatred, jealousy, bitterness, or envy. Then the love that you show that tough family member will allow him or her to be changed, and won over."

I raised my hand.

"Yes, Miss Yasmin."

"So, basically you are saying to just give it all to God: friendship issues and family issues. I guess I been doing that, and I still have issues."

"And that's not saying that you are doing anything wrong,

Yasmin. Keep on letting Him lead you and your path is going to be easier to walk. Guys and girls, just keep trusting God to be with you. He won't let you down. He's cheering for you to succeed in this life. Listen to Him and soak in all that applause from heaven."

⚜

I couldn't believe it was finally the first day of high school. It wouldn't be long before I'd be off to college somewhere, but yet I still don't know exactly what I want to do. I plan to take these four years and make sure my grades are consistently good. My mom had drilled into my mind over and over and over again that these are the grades that are going to count. I wouldn't get a chance to do them over. Colleges will look at my scores from ninth through twelfth grade, and I have to bring it. I'm ready to bring it. Who's going to rock my day? It's me, the Lord, and high school, baby. Yeah!

How about as soon as I set foot in this brand-new building I hear this group of girls talking about some pitiful female?

"She is not that cute," I heard one girl with a gruff voice say.

"I don't even know why he liked her in the first place. She's not all that with her tall, lanky self. She ain't even got no real curves."

"You better check her and let her know that he's your man," another girl said.

I was so glad that I had been in Sunday school the day before. I just wanted those girls to come up to me and talk about somebody so that I could set them straight. I mean, I wasn't going to jump in their conversation because they weren't talking to me, but they were being really mean and cruel. They could kill a girl's self-esteem by dogging her out the way they were doing.

What I gathered from all their information was that some girl had lost her boyfriend to another girl. And if that girl had the guy now, why did they care about the tall, lanky girl . . . wait a minute—tall, lanky?

I turned my head ninety degrees toward the really light-skinned one with the cute bob who said, "What you looking at? This is a free country; me and my friends can talk about you if we want too."

I was frozen. I couldn't believe what I was hearing. Wait, they were talking about me? Oh, so this was Myrek's new girl.

"She keeps staring at us like she thinks it's cool. Girl, please, you don't know us like that. You better turn them eyes to some-body else," one of them said to me.

All of a sudden, York and Myrek came up. My eyes must've been getting watery. I mean, they weren't making me cry or any-thing, but I was taken off guard. And maybe I was just a little hurt that Myrek really had someone else. I don't know what it was, but York knew that I was upset.

"What's going on? Somebody doing something to you, some-one saying something to you? Who I need to check?" he asked me.

I pulled him over to the side.

"I got it. I'm fine."

Then the girl threw her arms around Myrek and kissed him dead in the hallway. I saw him looking at me out the corner of his eye, but their lips were still locked and moving together.

"You gonna walk me to class, boo?" Raven asked Myrek.

"Naw, Raven. York and I got to go and see the basketball coach. I don't want to be showing affection all up in school and stuff. We could get in trouble."

"You know it felt good though, boo," she said, looking straight at me.

"You sure you all right?" York asked me.

"Yeah, I'm fine," I said.

Myrek and York left. Before I could even turn around and mind my own business, Raven and her three stooges got all up in my face.

"You see, that's my man, right? He likes me. His kisses were on me and I don't want to catch you nowhere around him. You just a goody two-shoes. You ain't ready to be a real woman and hold down a boyfriend no way."

I tried to step off to the side. I mean, what was she really saying? Okay, so maybe they had done more than kissing. And, so what? Good for them. It was none of my concern. That was Myrek's mistake, if you ask me.

They wouldn't let me out. They had boxed me in.

"Oh, what you scared? You trying to run off to class? You gonna hear what I have to say," Raven said.

"Yeah, you gonna hear what she has to say," the other girl said like a little parrot.

All of a sudden, Raven started getting really loud with me. Going off about what I was wearing, saying I wasn't that cute, calling me name after name. The Lord knew that I had just about taken enough of her stuff, and the "sweet" me was gone. I pushed Raven backwards so that she and I were face-to-face without her little goons around me.

"Let me just tell you something, honey, just so you understand real quick. If I wanted Myrek, he could be mine. I'm the one who put the brakes on where we were concerned. The little kiss you got from him or anything else you are talking about is only because I was done with that. And, I hope you really like him for who he is and not because he's a baller. If he breaks his leg, are you still going to be by his side? If the coach tells him that he can't play no more, are you still going to want to date him and kiss him then?

"Be real. Be a girl that's got some substance and not one that's just trying to be there for show. Call me names and threaten me all you want to, but Myrek's my boy and has been for a long time. If we have any kind of relationship, that's our business. It won't be something you can dictate, telling me how it will and won't go down. I think the worst mistake he made was getting with you. It won't last long."

I shoved her and went down the hall to look for my friends. One thing I could do was pray. *Lord, I'm sorry I got a little crazy, but shoot, she pushed me to the edge. She needed to know that she and her friends can't handle me any kind of way, right? Come on Lord, right?*

Perlicia and Asia came up to me at lunchtime.

"Oooh, it's going all around the school," Perlicia said.

"Raven wants to fight you," Asia said.

"Are you kidding?" I looked over at the two of them and said, "She and I already talked and, trust me, she don't want none of this. It ain't gonna be no fighting."

"No," Asia said. "They're telling everybody that after school it's gonna be the two of y'all. People saying they're going to miss the bus and everything. We got your back, girl. We know she got some girls who think they can fight. Veida's all caught in the middle because she knew them since middle school before she transferred to our school last year. So, she's trying to straddle the fence. I told her if she's on our side, if she's on our team, she's got your back, and then it ain't no choosing sides. I mean, she can't be on both sides. She got to be with us."

"You don't have to be with me. I'm not fighting anybody. You can spread the word that there ain't gonna be no fight," I said.

Perlicia grabbed my arm and said, "Listen, Miss Thing, you can't run away from a challenge. You got to show up. Let her be the one scared not to come. You got to be there."

"I don't gotta do nothing," I told her, removing her hand from my arm. "Look, I know y'all care about me, and I know y'all want my rep to stay good. We're girls and all, and if I look bad, y'all look bad. I understand that. I'm not crazy, but I'm not fighting nobody. It's not because I'm scared."

In my mind, I had really been wrestling with how I handled the situation with Raven earlier this morning anyway. I tried talking to God, trying to get Him to sign off on the fact that I was right. Would He be proud of the way I handled it? But, I didn't feel any confirmation about that. I didn't sense that I was correct in my actions. I actually felt more chastised.

This was exactly what Reverend Crane was talking about in Sunday school. I failed the test as soon as it was presented to me. But, I was going to have another chance since it was going around the school. It would be an even bigger audience. This was going to be my time to redeem myself. It was going to be my time to let the world know that God would fight my battles.

Yasmin Peace didn't have to step up there, twirling her head with her hands on her hips with the thought of getting ready to throw down. No, it wasn't going to go down like that. And nobody

was going to push me and make me want to go to blows with anybody over no boy, or for any other reason. Even though Myrek was
somebody I knew that I still cared about. Nuh uh.

I picked up my tray and went and sat by myself. I couldn't believe they kept pushing me to want to fight somebody. They were
my friends. Why would they possibly want me to get suspended
over some foolishness? It wasn't just about a rep that was mine.
They wanted me to look good, so that they could look good because they were my girls. Veida came over and sat down beside me.

"So, what are you going to do?" Veida asked.

"What do you mean, what am I going to do? I'm not going to
fight."

"I'm sorry, girl," she said.

"What? What are you talking about?" I asked.

"I guess I shouldn't have invited everybody to my party. We
weren't ready to merge. If I didn't have Raven and them there, they
wouldn't have met Myrek. He couldn't have dumped you to be with
her."

"Thanks for putting it like that," I said to my friend.

"I'm sorry. I just couldn't get it right," Veida said.

"Hmm, I'm sorry too," I told her.

Veida sounded pathetic. "All I wanted was somebody to care
about me, and I messed it up with York, Yancy, and Maurice. Now
I don't have nobody," Veida said. "That's why I sat beside you, you
know. We are the two miserable girls who are all alone with no
boys who like us."

"I'm cool with that," I told her quickly.

"No, you're not. You lookin' all sad over here too, Yasmin."

"No, I'm not. I'm just trying to eat my lunch and I'm just sick and tired of everybody telling me how I should feel, what I should feel, and what I should do."

"All right, all right, calm down. It's cool being alone," Veida said.

"I'm not alone. You're sitting right here, Veida. When is having a good girlfriend not good enough? I'm just a ninth grader. I just got to high school," I explained.

"Look, I'm cool and you got it going on. So, I guess you need to be cool too," Veida said.

"Forget my brothers, forget Maurice—it's their loss. They don't want to talk to you right now because you don't know which one you really want to give your full attention to. Just chill. Find out who you are. Let's get into our books. Let's get some As. You know?"

"Yeah, yeah, I guess you got a point," Veida added.

Just when I felt like I was gaining some ground, I heard Raven say, "Oh, so you don't want to fight me? You scared, huh?"

Suddenly, the small table where Veida and I were sitting became the center of attention. All kinds of people started stepping toward us.

"No, I'm not going to fight you."

"Told y'all she was scared." Raven started doing a little dance and the crowd was getting hyped.

"I'm not going to fight you—not because I'm scared of you but —because I want to please God."

I looked over and saw York on one side and Yancy on another. They knew what I was talking about. They knew I had to take the high road and I didn't care if anybody didn't understand it. But I certainly had to explain it.

This was my opportunity and I was ready. "Raven, you already won. You are Myrek's girlfriend. We don't need to fight over that. You said I'm lame because I don't want to give it up. I'm not trying to please anybody here. I'm just trying to make the Guy upstairs happy. And as long as He's in my heart and I follow His rules, you can think I'm lame, you can think I'm a punk, you can think I'm whatever. Those are just words that don't hurt me."

I was laying it all out for her. "This is the first day of school, Raven. I don't need a beef with you because if I'm trying to represent anyone it's not my brothers, it's not my girls, it's not Myrek, it's God. I'm here on His team trying to make Him proud. I'm not going to fight you. I'm God's number one fan."

Chapter 12

Offer
Only Happiness

*T*he first week of school flew by. Ever since I'd gotten over the incident that happened on the first day with Raven and her crew, I had respect and I didn't even put up one fist. I just lifted up God.

I had so many people come to me and telling me how they loved the Lord. Or, they asked me how I was so strong in my faith. The Lord equipped me with stuff to say and I was praying for people who had issues that I knew only God could solve. Before the week was over, they were coming to me with testimonies about the Lord showing up and showing out. It was all-good.

I wasn't trying to be a missionary at school, but I knew God called us to be fishers of men. Basically, that meant we are supposed to tell folks about who He is and that we can trust Him to take care of us. Then He'd do the rest in our lives, in our hearts, and in our souls. I was so excited to see that happening firsthand.

When we all focused on Jesus more, the things that weighed us down didn't seem so bad at all.

⚜

Later Friday night, I was in my bedroom sleeping and I heard Mom say in a loud tone, "John, I told you, I don't want any part in that. Jeffery got himself into all this, and I just want me and my kids to be left alone. I mean, you can go down there if you want to. You can try to help him out, but don't ask me to join you. And, please, don't lay any guilt trips on me. I didn't get Jeffery into that foolishness, and I'm not tryin' to speak on his behalf."

"But, you just don't understand. It helps when someone going up for parole has a family there who cares. You're his family," Uncle John tried to reason with her.

I got up out of my bed and opened the door. Mom was saying that she didn't want me and my brothers to help my dad get out of jail. I didn't really know how I felt about that. I mean, sure I'd be nervous getting up and having to testify, but how could I not do it? How could we not say anything? How could we not be there for my father? I looked to the right and noticed that both of my brothers were in the hallway listening too. So instead of me just peeking, I opened up the door and stepped out into the hallway with them.

York whispered, "I don't care what she says. I'm goin' with Uncle John. I'm goin' to help. Dad's finally got a chance to get out, and she's sayin' that we can't help. Naw, that ain't even right."

"You can't be disrespectful," Yancy said, trying not to let Mom know that we were listening. "That's what's wrong with you. You're always trying to do your own thing regardless of what Ma says."

"Man, that's not true," York started to argue.

"You know what, you two? I am so sick of y'all always fussing. Thinking the both of y'all are so big and bad and know everything that's going on, like you know all the answers," I said impatiently.

"What are y'all fussing about? It's midnight and I'm having a personal conversation. And I know y'all are not listening in!" Mom shouted, busting all three of us.

"See, Yvette, they want to come," Uncle John said, taking advantage of the moment.

None of us, not even Yancy had said that we didn't. I could see by my mother's eyes that she was feeling hurt, but she wasn't going to take that desire away from us.

"They wanna go, fine. We'll go," she said. And that was the end of that. We packed our bags and drove down that night.

The parole hearing was at nine on Saturday morning. I hoped York was checking out all the steel bars and guard gates we had to get through. The way he was living, he needed to know that if he didn't straighten up his ways, he could end up in this very place. I checked out Yancy when he saw Dad come in with handcuffs on. I could tell a part of him was sympathetic that his father had to live that way.

After the people who worked with my father got up and said such positive things, my Uncle John said a whole bunch of nice stuff too. The judge asked if anybody else in the family had anything to say.

"We just want him out," York blurted before Mom popped him.

"That not what you do, that's not how you act," she scolded.

"Well, young man, if you'd like to say something please come up and address the whole committee."

Yancy touched his shoulder and said, "No, I'll go."

"You're gonna say something?" York asked surprised.

"I got this, man. I'm going to talk." York looked over at me like he was thinking, *I hope he ain't gon' mess this up for Dad.* Yancy smiled at Mom and somehow I felt relieved. Before he had even said a word, I knew it was going to be powerful.

Yancy began. "I got to be honest, judge. I've been the one in my family who's been estranged from my father for years. But even though he's been locked up, he's tried to keep in contact with all of us, and he's done a pretty good job with it. I guess I just didn't realize until recently how much I suffer because I don't have him there. I don't think it's going to be instant that we will have a real father-and-son relationship, like a good bond and stuff automatically. But I know if he stays here, there's no way he can help me be the kind of man that won't end up here."

He was on a roll as he continued to convince the committee. "My brother, York, loves him to pieces. And honestly, judge, my dad needs to be out to make sure York has the kind of tough love that only a father can give, so he stays on the right course too. And my sister, Yasmin, she's starting to like these boys and stuff and they're starting to like her. Yeah, we need our dad to be home."

"And, what about your mom? Your parents are divorced. You know, there's no guarantee that you guys will be under the same roof," the judge inquired.

"But if he's out, judge, we've got a shot to make life better that we haven't had in years. Just give us that chance. Don't keep our father away from us any longer. We've lost one sibling, and we all need each other to really heal from that," Yancy responded.

A couple of the committee members had tears in their eyes.

My mom cried. They agreed to let Dad out, but he couldn't move to Jacksonville until he found a job there. He hugged us all. I really felt that the connection we all shared was anointed by God.

It was awkward during the times when Mom and Dad were together. They didn't say too much to each other, even though she had seemed excited on the day he was released. Dad had wanted us to stay down there so we could celebrate together, and Mom wanted us to get back home so we'd be ready for school. It wasn't big tension but it wasn't all good.

Two weeks later, we were at home doing our thing. Mom was out with Mr. Mike. And, as much as I wanted her to quit all of that, I guess she was going to do it her way.

I was so shocked to see my brothers studying at the kitchen table. I mean, not that I was surprised to see Yancy studying. I mean, he was a bookworm. As hard as he tried to step away from it and act like he wanted a different game, he was just naturally gifted when it came to academics. Now he was even helping York out. And the way he was explaining algebra, breaking it down, and making it cool, York was getting it and they were laughing.

That prompted me to say, "Okay, so now we're all one big, happy family?"

"Sit down, little sis," York said, pushing back one of the chairs.

"We're always a family. We're brothers. We're not going to get along all the time, but that doesn't mean I don't still love the boy even when I say that I can't stand him," Yancy said.

"Yeah, ditto for me," York said. "I was really glad when Yancy stepped up to the plate and said what he said about Dad. I dunno know. It just did somethin' for our relationship."

"Well, you know my girl Veida still likes both of y'all," I said.

York said, "When she was with me, she just kept talkin' 'bout Yancy. She don't really like me."

"Why didn't you tell me that, man?" Yancy asked.

"I don't know." I reached over and jabbed York in the arm.

"Owww. You know my arm is still sore," York said. And that just reminded me again that we had been through so much. It had only been a few months since the fire and though we'd had one crazy summer, we were all on one accord. We loved each other and we were going to stick it out. We were going to make sure that we were there for each other. We would live up to our name and be a peaceful family.

Suddenly, we heard a knock at the door and then Uncle John's voice. "Open up in here."

"You got some food?" York yelled and opened the door. We were all amazed to see not only Uncle John, but he was standing there with our father. York dashed into his arms. Yancy stood back and acted reserved. When York ushered him in, I got my big hug.

"Hey, baby girl, you handling these jokers?"

"Trying to keep them in check, Daddy," I said, "you know I'm the only good one."

"Yeah, I know," he joked.

"Dad, what are you doing here?" York asked.

"Oh, you not happy to see me? We do have food, soul food." My uncle handed two bags to me, and I put them in the kitchen.

"All right, I'll be back in what, an hour or so?" Uncle John asked Dad.

"Yeah, that sounds good, John," he replied. Uncle John said that he'd see us all later and left.

"Oh, by the way," Dad said to us, "I'll be workin' on a delivery truck, so I got a work permit to be up here. Boy, did I miss y'all kids. What's going on with you three?"

We all sat down at the table and just started talking to our dad about everything. York and I noticed that Yancy was quiet and so, instead of us hoarding all of Dad's time, we let the two of them communicate some. It was actually working pretty well.

Daddy talked about how happy he was to have a granddaughter and was glad that Uncle John and Aunt Lucinda had adopted her.

Then the knob on the door turned. We hadn't even talked about where Mom was. I guess Dad just assumed she was at work. She got off her job around six and now it was ten. When she opened the door, there stood Mr. Mike right behind her. Dad stood to his feet and so did York and Yancy. I just laid my head down on the table and prayed, *Lord, be with us.*

Dad went over and said, "Hey, I'm Jeffery, the kids' father. Sorry for just showing up like this, Yvette. Um, John brought me by. He'll be back in just a few minutes."

"Oh no, you and the kids are fine," Mom said.

"No, I'm going to step out," Mr. Mike said.

"Yvette, thanks for a great evening. Hey man, it's nice to meet you. Your kids are excited you're back."

It was hardcore, but it was all good. Nobody talked about who was going to have Mom's heart in the end. I mean, it wasn't time for any of that, but it was time for us to act like things could be worked out. Thankfully, that's just what we did.

Mr. Mike left and Mom went to her room. Dad finished talking to us until Uncle John came back to pick him up. Although it
wasn't a perfect night, we were on a course for healing. Dad and Mr.
Mike were both Angel's grandfathers, so it would help if they got
along. Who could ask for anything more?

⊰⊱

"Hey, Veida, wait up," I said when I saw her in school the next
day.

"Hey, girl," she said to me, "you're getting all popular and everything, Yasmin. Everybody in the ninth grade wants to talk to you."

"Girl, please," I said.

"I'm just saying," Veida said, "it's so nice to know you're standing for Him."

"We don't have any classes together, Veida, so I know it seems
like we haven't hung out a lot," I said.

"You didn't even come to the last modeling session," she said.

"Yeah, I know. We had to go down and see my dad. I plan on
making it to the next one, though. You know, we should try out for
the dance team too."

"Oh, that would be cool, either that or the step team," Veida
said. "I miss you, Yasmin."

"I miss you too. York was telling Yancy that when you two were
together you were still talking about Yancy a lot."

"I kept putting my foot in my mouth. I think that's when York
said, 'You know what, I'm not fooling with you no more.'"

"I sort of thought you were going back and forth between the
two of them."

"I thought I was too, but I guess my mind was where I really knew who had my heart."

"Why didn't you tell me?" I asked.

"Because, I was with Yancy and then with York. Then, to tell you that I wanted to be with Yancy again—I don't know. It just felt kind of dumb, even to me."

"Well, I just want to let you know that I still stand behind what I said. You got it going on, talking about modeling, being on the dance team. Now that the boys are out of our hands, we don't have to chase nobody, and it's all good with us being God's girls. You know what I'm saying?" I said to encourage her.

"Yeah, I hear you, Yasmin. I've been praying every night, you know. Praying for my family, praying for me to be strong and to not think about the tack-head jokers as much."

"Has it been working, Veida?"

"Yeah, I've also been praying for me and you to be close again. For you to stop me in the hall like this, it's working more than I know."

"Good," I said.

"All right, I got to get to class," Veida said.

"Cool, girl," I said waving.

As I walked to French class, Raven came over to me and said, "I am so sick of you coming between my relationship with Myrek. Everybody around here is talking about how high and mighty you are and what a good girl you are. You ain't fooling nobody with all this God talk, like you better than the rest of us or something."

"Raven, what are you talkin' about?" I asked, continuing to walk on, not even wanting to stop and give her the time of day.

"I'm talking to you," she said, grabbing my arm and yanking me to look at her.

I let that go. "Okay, you've got my full attention. What do you want to say?" I asked.

"I'm just saying, you walk around here thinking you're better than everybody. Myrek mumbles and talks about you from time to time. As if I should be nice like you and have deep conversations with him about you. I'm so sick of him talking about you that I could puke all over you. You need to go and get a life. If God is so in your corner, how could He let your brother commit suicide? Or your Dad be in jail most of your life?"

"The Lord gives and the Lord takes away, Raven. Just because I have bad stuff happening to me doesn't mean that He doesn't love me or He doesn't care."

"I'm just so sick—" She started pointing her finger in my face. Before I could step away, Myrek came between the two of us.

"Raven, what are you doing?" Myrek asked.

"Oh, nothing, boo," she said, backing off.

"Wait a minute, I just heard you. You were talking about her brother and her dad. You know what?—"

"Oh no, you don't understand, Myrek. Tell him, Yasmin. Tell him I didn't say anything like that."

"I don't need her to lie. I heard you. But I don't even want a girl like that," Myrek told her.

"What do you mean? You saying you're breaking up with me? I'm just sick and tired of you talking about her. That's all. And, I'm telling her to stay out of our face."

"Well, there is no 'our face' to stay out of. You're a cool girl, Raven, but you're just not the one for me. It's over." She started whining to him as he talked to her.

I just turned around and let the two of them have it. I couldn't

Offer Only Happiness   151

believe I had witnessed a breakup, and it did affect me in some kind
of way. But, I had moved on. I had put my attention on things
above. I was able to say to a girl who had verbally attacked me that
God did care about me. And, if I'd had more time, I would've told
her that He cared about her too.

"Hey, can you wait up?" Myrek asked me.

"It seems like you've got business to finish," I said.

"Didn't you hear me? That's that. I'm sorry she was so rude like
that."

"It's your fault, you know," I told him.

"What? What are you talking about, Yasmin? I didn't make
her say nothing like that."

I took my hand and placed it on his lips. "Shhh, I know that.
What I'm saying is that she said you kept talking about me. You
can't do that to girls, and you can't do that to guys either," I said, re-
membering how Veida had bruised York's ear when she talked to
him about Yancy.

"I was trying to be all tough and stuff, Yasmin, thinking that
our friendship didn't matter to me. I know that I can't really ask
you to forgive me. But, I can tell that we're growing. It's changing
so much."

"You are fine," I said.

"I am kind of fine, ain't I? See my muscles growing?"

"Oh, you are silly. Got jokes and everything," I said, teasing
him.

"I guess what I'm saying is, I just want to be in your life again.
Is that's okay? Not no boyfriend and girlfriend thing, not right off
the bat or whatever, but be my best friend again. I miss you, Yasmin."
I smiled and we hugged.

When I went to class and sat there waiting for the teacher to arrive, I just thought about all that had gone on over the summer. And though everything wasn't the way I wanted it to be, I knew that God was working. And I could count it all joy.

I was growing and I had to be prepared so that if I went through something, it was okay. God didn't say that my days here were going to be easy, but He did tell me that if I did things His way, I'd have a bright future.

Now, I know that joy isn't just about feeling good. Rather, it is a mental state of consciously wanting to look at the good in all things and—offer only happiness.

Acknowledgments

*H*ere is a thank-you to those who help me along the way. We need each other to keep going.

For my family, parents Dr. Franklin and Shirley Perry, Sr., and brother, Dennis, and sister-in-law, Leslie, my mother-in-law, Ms. Ann, and extended family, Rev. Walter and Marjorie Kimbrough, Bobby and Sarah Lundy, Antonio and Gloria London, Cedric and Nicole Smith, Harry and Nino Colon, and Brett and Loni Perriman, you constant cheering keeps me moving even when life gets tough.

For my publisher, Moody/Lift Every Voice, and especially Karen Waddles, your faith to not give up on me keeps me not giving up on myself.

For my eighth-grade friends, Veida Evans, Kimberly Brickhouse Monroe, Joy Barksdale Nixon, Jan Hatchett, Vickie Randall Davis, and my new family, Tina Crittenden and Angela King, your friendship keeps me knowing I'm blessed.

For my attorney, Michele Clark Davis, your guidance keeps me hanging on to the fact that I'm just a contract away from greatness.

For my children, Dustyn Leon, Sydni Derek, and Sheldyn Ashli, your being part of my life keeps me filled.

For my husband, Derrick Moore, your heart you give to me daily keeps me pursuing all that is out there for us to share.

For my readers, truly those of you who daily live in rough situations, your life concerns keeps me writing to let you know it's not so bad after all.

And for my God, who blessed me with many joys—Your unending love keeps me thankful.

Discussion Questions

1. Yasmin Peace's brother is recovering from a fire burn, and the hospital bills are so expensive that her mother doesn't know what she will do. Do you think it is good that the neighborhood wanted to help pay? What are some other things people can do to help those who go through a tough situation?

2. Jada isn't sure that she wants to give her baby up. Do you think it is okay to change her mind? Explain times when you have been torn over your decisions and how God helped you figure out what was best.

3. In the L.I.G.H.T. group meeting there is a discussion about self-esteem and true joy. Do you think Yasmin walked away from the meeting feeling better about herself? What does true joy mean to you?

4. At Veida's pool party Myrek and Yasmin get very close. Do you agree with Myrek getting upset with Yasmin when she pulls away? What are appropriate boundaries that should be set in a relationship between teens?

5. Yasmin visits her grandmother and learns that she may have Alzheimer's. Do you think Yasmin's aunt made the right decision in sending her grandmother to a home? When you don't agree with decisions that are made, what are suitable ways to address your concerns?

6. Alyssa, Yasmin's cousin, is involved with illegal activities to make a quick dollar. Do you think Yasmin was right to lead her aunt to Alyssa? Do you believe the Lord wants you to help others get out of trouble?

7. Yasmin's mom is upset that she didn't know Yasmin went to visit her father. Do you think Yasmin was right to keep the whole truth from her mom? Why is it important to be honest with our parents?

8. Yasmin goes to a great youth rally. What do you think was the message of the event? Why is going to church important?

9. Myrek has a new girlfriend. Do you think Yasmin handled the news well? Can you maintain a friendship when you don't like what the other person is doing?

10. Yasmin's Uncle John and Aunt Lucinda have wanted a family for many years. How do you think they felt finally getting to love on three children? Do you think God gives us blessings in ways we can't imagine? If so, explain.

11. Asia and Perlicia want to fight Raven for messing with Yasmin. Do you think Yasmin was right to squash it all and walk away from the tension? What are ways to deal with people who are not nice?

12. Yasmin's dad gets parole. Do you think this is good for the family? How can God take a bad situation and make something great still happen?

FINDING YOUR FAITH

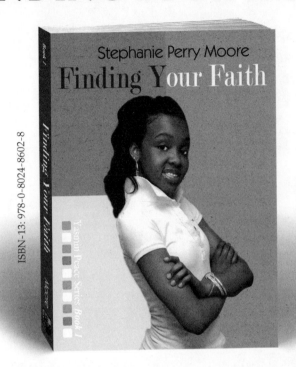

ISBN-13: 978-0-8024-8602-8

Yasmin Peace is growing up fast. After the tragic suicide of her oldest brother, she takes on the responsibility of overseeing what's left of her family and through it all, she perseveres. As she sheds her tomboy exterior and finds her faith, Yasmin blossoms into the young lady God destined her to become. Join Yasmin Peace on her journey through this series that will encourage character growth and development.

WWW.LIFTEVERYVOICEBOOKS.COM

1-800-678-8812 · MOODYPUBLISHERS.COM

BELIEVING IN HOPE

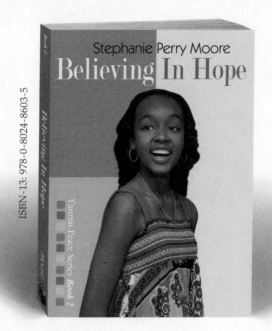

In this second book of the Yasmin Peace series, family tensions and school unrest soar to a fever pitch. A school counselor begins the LIGHT club, a club dedicated to helping eighth grade girls deal with issues like gangs, depression, teen suicide, and self esteem. Yasmin discovers that there is hope on the other side of every obstacle—if she holds on to her faith.

WWW.LIFTEVERYVOICEBOOKS.COM

1-800-678-8812 · MOODYPUBLISHERS.COM

THE PAYTON SKKY SERIES

From her senior year of high school to her second semester of college, this series traces the life of Payton Skky, showing how this lively and energetic teenager's faith is challenged as she faces tough issues.

The Negro National Anthem

Lift every voice and sing
Till earth and heaven ring,
Ring with the harmonies of Liberty;
Let our rejoicing rise
High as the listening skies,
Let it resound loud as the rolling sea.
Sing a song full of the faith that the dark past has taught us,
Sing a song full of the hope that the present has brought us,
Facing the rising sun of our new day begun
Let us march on till victory is won.

So begins the Black National Anthem, by James Weldon Johnson in 1900. Lift Every Voice is the name of the joint imprint of The Institute for Black Family Development and Moody Publishers.

Our vision is to advance the cause of Christ through publishing African-American Christians who educate, edify, and disciple Christians in the church community through quality books written for African Americans.

Since 1988, the Institute for Black Family Development, a 501(c)(3) non-profit Christian organization, has been providing training and technical assistance for churches and Christian organizations. The Institute for Black Family Development's goal is to become a premier trainer in leadership development, management, and strategic planning for pastors, ministers, volunteers, executives, and key staff members of churches and Christian organizations. To learn more about The Institute for Black Family Development write us at:

The Institute for Black Family Development
15151 Faust
Detroit, Michigan 48223

We hope you enjoy this book from Moody Publishers. Our goal is to provide high-quality, thought-provoking books and products that connect truth to your real needs and challenges. For more information on other books and products written and produced from a biblical perspective, go to www.moodypublishers.com or write to:

Moody Publishers/LEV
820 N. LaSalle Boulevard
Chicago, IL 60610
www.moodypublishers.com